RUMRUNNERS

MARK PARRAGH

Waterhaven MEDIA

Rumrunners
by Mark Parragh

A Waterhaven Media Publication
First Print Edition – October, 2019

Cover Design by Shayne Rutherford, Wicked Good Book Covers
Editing and Production Coordination by Nina Sullivan

CONTENTS

NASSAU, BAHAMAS, 1924

The sound was what Colin loved most. It was a frothy combination of voices, clinking glasses, and women's laughter that drifted lightly on the air. It seemed to weave its way among the casino's glittering lights and settle gently on the shoulders of Colin's dinner jacket. It was always in the background as he considered his chips and studied the faces of the other players at the table. It felt like listening to the casino's heartbeat. He could tell when people were winning, feel the swings in their moods. It was a pleasant place, and a pleasant sound. It was better than the dreariness back home anyway.

And it was a hell of a lot better than the Somme.

"Your bet, Ridley. Come on."

Colin looked up and smiled. It was Dempsey who'd spoken. His family was in steel and manufacturing. Around him were the tuxedoed sons of American financial and industrial might. Cooke, banking in Philadelphia. Crocker, railroads in the west. Hopkins, railroads in the east. Hill, coal and oil. Bartlett, cattle. They were all college pals in their early twenties, and between them they represented enough money to buy the Bahamas outright. They enjoyed playing cards with a charming young Englishman. And no matter how much he took off them, they could just wire home for more.

But it was Dempsey who was looking at him with eager anticipation. Dempsey who was hoping to claw back some of his losses because he thought he had the strong hand. Colin glanced down at his cards and decided Dempsey was probably right.

"I'm out," he said with a hint of dismay and dropped his cards on the table. There was a wave of irritated muttering, a flurry of flipped cards, and Dempsey won the hand with a straight.

"I don't understand," Dempsey said as he raked in the pot. "I win a hand, I win fifty bucks. You win, you win a thousand. What's your secret, Ridley? Did you pay off a witch doctor or something?"

"Just born lucky," he said. "How I made it through the war."

Of course, it didn't hurt that he was also considerably better at poker. For all their money and status and the style that came so effortlessly to them, none of these young Americans could play cards worth a damn. Any fool could draw a good hand and bet hard on it. But that was all they seemed to know how to do. They had no idea how to read the table, when to go in heavy and when to back off a hand. Everything had always come so easily. They seemed to assume that all they had to do was throw money on the table and more money would naturally come back to them. At least when they lost, it was just a curiosity. They'd happily throw more money after it all night.

Colin checked his watch. It was nearly ten. "And now, I'm afraid I must bid you goodnight, gentlemen," he said, gathering up his chips. "Prior engagement. But I'll be here tomorrow night if you'd like a chance to win your money back."

"Bloody hell, Ridley," said Crocker, who had lately begun to affect an unconvincing British accent. "Not very sporting."

Colin smiled. "Sorry, can't be helped. By the way, where's Endicott? Haven't seen him all night. Thought he'd be here."

"Radiotelegraph office," said Cooke, opening his cigarette case. "Burning up the airwaves to New York. Some family confab he couldn't get out of. He said he'd be joining us later."

"All right," said Colin, "give him my best."

He smiled as he headed to the cashier's cage to redeem his chips. It had been a good night, and it was about to get better. Endicott would be the last of them to leave the casino on an early night. If he was starting late tonight, he'd probably close the place down. And aboard Endicott's very expensive yacht, his girlfriend Phoebe would be all alone, waiting.

The night air was warm and humid as Colin stepped out of the Bahamian Club, but the breeze off the harbor was refreshing. A thunderstorm had passed through earlier, and the street was spattered with patches of water. A police officer nodded to Colin as he passed. Gambling was illegal in the Bahamas, but the Bahamian Club catered exclusively to well-off foreigners, mainly British expats and American tourists, and so it was quietly tolerated.

Colin whistled to himself as he made his way down to the waterfront, anticipation putting a little bounce in his step. These rich young Americans weren't just bad at cards; they also tended to take their women for granted, leaving them at loose ends while they gambled and caroused in Nassau's playgrounds. He could take more than money off of them.

Colin turned beside a rowdy fisherman's bar and made his way to the slips. These were an improvised maze of docks that snaked out from the main wharf. They'd been built out in fits and starts as traffic increased, leaving narrow channels out into the main harbor. Moored alongside them were a diverse fleet of pleasure craft—the working boats moored farther up the wharf. There was everything from small racing boats to enormous steam yachts belonging to millionaires.

Colin's own boat, *Pegasus*, was docked at the far end of one of these. She was a Gar Wood design: mahogany hull powered by a

Napier Lion engine and capable of deceptive speed and maneuverability for a boat her size. She was Colin's proudest possession, the one that drank up most of the money he won from wealthy tourists. But he wasn't heading for *Pegasus* tonight. Instead, he took a left where the dock branched, and made his way around to Endicott's two-masted racing yacht, *Camille*. She wasn't a bad boat—Endicott could afford the best after all—but she was rigged and furnished indifferently. Endicott wanted a boat because the code of his social circle dictated that a rich young man like him should have one. He had little idea what to actually do with it once it was purchased.

But the *Camille* did have one redeeming quality, Colin saw as he approached. One long, silken lady's glove hung over the port rail. It was their prearranged signal. The way was clear.

Colin hurried up the narrow gangplank onto the deck and listened at the aft companionway. He heard nothing from below, so he slipped down the steep stairs and along the passageway to the master suite.

As his eyes adjusted, Colin saw a form beneath the bedclothes that gleamed in the pale light from the portholes. He heard soft, gentle breathing. It sounded like Phoebe had fallen asleep waiting for him. That was remedied easily enough.

"Hello, darling," he murmured as he knelt on the bedside. "Did you miss me?"

Suddenly the cabin lights clicked on, and the figure in bed sat up. Endicott.

Oh, hell. Not good. Not good at all.

"Hullo Ridley," said Endicott. "Out for a nighttime stroll, are we?"

"Endicott! I…"

Endicott was fully dressed in linen shirt and canvas slacks. He rolled off the bed and gave Colin a dark, humorless grin. "Had to send Phoebe home, I'm afraid. Turns out she couldn't be trusted."

"Look, Endicott," Colin stammered, backing out of the cabin

into the passageway. "This isn't what you think at all. There's a perfectly reasonable explanation!"

Endicott followed Colin as he backed away. "Of course, there is," he said. "Dying to hear it."

Colin's mind raced, grasping at threads, but they all melted away into nothing the instant he put any weight on them. He took another step back and felt his foot hit the bottom step of the companionway.

"Yeah, okay," he said finally. "I've got nothing."

Then he turned and hurled himself up the steps to the main deck...and stopped dead. There was Cooke, as well as Dempsey, Crocker, all of them. They stood in a loose circle on the deck, with Hopkins guarding the mouth of the gangplank. Dempsey had removed his dinner jacket and was rolling up his sleeves.

"Stealing another fellow's girl? Not something a gentleman does," said Cooke.

"Definitely conduct unbecoming," Endicott added as he emerged from below decks behind Colin.

"And if you'd do that, we have to wonder what else you're capable of," said Dempsey. "All those nights cleaning us out at the table."

"Hey!" Colin snapped. He stepped forward and poked Dempsey in the chest with an index finger. "I do *not* cheat at cards!"

He glanced at the rail as Dempsey grabbed his outstretched hand.

"I don't hear you denying the rest of it," Endicott snapped.

"Well, that can't be helped," he said. "It's the accent. Drives girls mad."

Then Colin grabbed Dempsey's wrist with his free hand and spun him around. Dempsey squawked as he lost his balance. These fellows couldn't play cards, they couldn't keep a woman, and they sure as hell hadn't spent any time in brutal hand-to-hand trench fighting with the German army. He threw Dempsey into Cooke beside him, then dashed through the opening he'd made. He vaulted the rail and fell down to the dock below. He landed in a crouch on the wooden planks, then sprang to his feet and dashed away as the gang of angry young millionaires shouted their outrage and hurried after him.

Colin turned a corner and sprinted past the fork that led to shore. Instead he angled left and hurried past several smaller powerboats and a two-masted cruising schooner. *Pegasus* was moored at the end of this dock. It would be best if he left Nassau behind for a while, he thought, and let things cool down.

But then he saw that Endicott and his gang had put more planning into this little ambush than he'd thought. A figure stood at the end of the dock—a large, muscular young man in a suit. Behind him, *Pegasus* had been cut loose and was drifting out into the open harbor.

Oh, hell.

Colin pulled up. His boat slowly turned in the gentle current, well beyond the distance he could jump. He and the other man considered each other for a moment.

"Football?" Colin asked at last.

"Left Guard," the young man said with a proud grin. "Just made All-American."

"Really? Congratulations," said Colin. "Well, best get to it, I suppose."

Instantly the man was charging him, bent forward, his muscled legs propelling him down the dock like a steam locomotive. Colin had to admit he was fast, and he was sure he was very effective against the Yale defensive line. But Colin wasn't a football player.

He went low, beneath the arms reaching for him, and spun. The man's momentum carried him onto Colin's back, and Colin thrust up hard with both legs, and then threw him off the side of the dock. The All-American went into the harbor with a surprised yelp and an impressive splash.

Colin gave *Pegasus* a longing look, but there was no way to reach her. Instead he turned and rushed back down the dock, hoping he could reach the turnoff before he was cut off

But he was too late, he saw as he rounded the corner. His pursuers had reached the fork and were bearing down on him. He was cornered.

In desperation, Colin looked around and spotted the schooner he'd passed on the way down. The gangplank was extended so he dashed back and ran up to the deck. Immediately he heard someone rustling below, and Endicott and his gang were nearly to the gangplank. In desperation, Colin leapt onto the rail and climbed up into the rigging.

"What the hell's going on up here?" someone shouted. "Get down from there or I'll shoot you down!"

Colin looked down to the deck. An older man in pajamas and a robe was looking up at him, waving a pistol. This was starting to not be fun anymore. At least the pistol had intimidated Endicott and the others. They'd stopped cold at the bottom of the gangplank and watched him climb into the rigging with amazement. But he was still treed. He needed a way out of here now. A line slung from the mainmast hung beside him. Colin grabbed it and looked across the narrow channel separating this row of slips from the next. On the other side was a Bermuda-rigged ketch. About sixty feet away from the look of it. Well, if it didn't work, the result would be a drop into the harbor that would ruin his tuxedo. He was facing a lot worse than that. As the boat's angry master aimed at him, Colin took a breath and then hurled himself from the rigging.

He heard the gun go off with a roar as he swung down across the deck and over the rail. Then he released the rope and for a moment flew above the dark harbor. He caught himself in the ketch's shroud lines and nearly wrenched one arm from its socket. He grunted in pain, then started clambering down.

Across the channel, the old man was still shouting at him. But he hadn't fired again. Endicott and his gang were running back down the docks. Colin dropped the last few feet to the deck, then dashed down the gangplank and raced them back toward the shore. When he reached the wharf, he turned left and sprinted along the waterfront with the mob hot behind him.

This is ridiculous, he thought. *I'm getting chased around Nassau harbor by the Harvard class of '23.*

Then he saw a boat approaching the wharf. It was a steam-powered wooden fishing boat with flaking white paint. Its pilot looked up at him.

"Colin? Colin Ridley!"

Marcus? Here?

He looked again. Yes, that was Marcus, one of the foremen on his family's farm. Colin had no idea what Marcus was doing here, but this was no time to question a rescue.

"Marcus!" he shouted, gesturing wildly. "Pull alongside!"

Marcus maintained speed and steered the boat as close to the pilings as he dared. With one last look over his shoulder, Colin leaped and tumbled into the boat. Marcus turned sharply, and the boat moved out into the harbor. Endicott and his companions were left shouting and gesturing from the wharf.

"Yes!" Colin shouted at Marcus. "Thanks, Marcus! Bit of luck, you showing up like this."

"Nothing lucky about it—" Marcus began.

"No, no, go back," Colin interrupted. "The bastards cut *Pegasus* loose. She's drifting out into the channel."

Marcus shook his head. "Harbor patrol will tow her in. You're going to Beckers Cay."

"Damn it, Marcus, I told them I'm not—"

"It's your mother!" the old Bahamian snapped. "She's taken ill. She maybe passed already. Your brother sent me to bring you home. Thought it'd take longer to find you, but you're damn well going home. Now sit down!"

Stunned, Colin settled back onto a small wooden bench near the pilot column.

"Okay," he said, "okay," and he watched the grim determination on Marcus's weathered face as he steered the boat back out to sea.

Beckers Cay. Home. Colin hadn't been back in more than a year. And he hadn't really lived there since the war. He'd cut himself off as effectively as he could. But mother...Marcus was right. No getting out of it. He had to go.

The boat's engine puttered a steady rhythm as it headed into the dark waters.

Talk about going from the frying pan into the fire.

_____

2

DAWN WAS JUST BEGINNING TO GLOW IN THE EASTERN SKY AS THEY reached Beckers Cay. Colin had grown up on this tiny spit of sand and sea grass at the outer fringe of the Bahamas. He had no idea what had lured his father out here in the waning days of the last century, to grow sisal of all things. But it was home, for better or worse.

Worse, usually.

As they entered the island's small natural harbor, Colin saw fishing boats run up on the beach. Another boat was moored to the dock.

"Doctor MacAllen," said Marcus. "He made it. Good."

Colin had asked Marcus what had happened to his mother, but Marcus had been dispatched to Nassau before the doctor arrived. All he knew was that she'd suddenly collapsed.

Marcus cut the engine, and they glided alongside the dock. Colin leaped across the gap, tied off the bow line, and helped Marcus up. No one was here to meet them. They walked up the trail toward the main house.

The place looked even worse than Colin remembered. The

fields on either side of him were sandy and bare. On the far side, wild plants were starting to creep back into the cleared land.

"Stephen didn't plant this year?" he asked.

"Not here," said Marcus. "A few acres on the north side. Not enough to keep the men busy. No money anyway. Most of them gone back to fishing."

So the farm was failing. Colin wasn't surprised. Their father might have looked at this land and seen riches, but that was a long time ago.

The family home was a two-story Georgian Revival pile his father had built in the early days of his optimism. Now it was sagging and badly in need of repair. Even a fresh coat of paint would help, but he imagined Stephen had bigger problems to deal with.

People milled around the front yard. Small bonfires burned low. They'd been out here all night, keeping vigil. Faces turned as he approached, and someone ran in to announce his arrival.

"Don't you worry," a man said as Colin passed. "She's a strong woman, Miss Emily. She'll make it through."

"I hope you're right," said Colin. "I don't know what's happened."

"Nobody's saying," a woman added nearby. "I think they're waiting for you."

"I'll tell you as soon as I know something," he promised, raising his voice for the crowd.

Then he stopped at the bottom of the porch steps. In the open doorway stood his younger brother, Stephen. They weren't twins, but no one could doubt they were brothers. Both had the distinctive family eyes and long, narrow nose. Colin's hair was dark while Stephen's was a sandy blonde, but otherwise they looked like the same subject drawn by different artists.

They looked at each other in silence for a long moment. Then Stephen brushed his hair from his forehead and said, "You better come up."

Inside, Stephen led the way through the main hall. It didn't look like the home of a prosperous country gentleman anymore. They must have been selling off the antiques.

"How is she?" Colin asked softly.

"She's had a stroke," said Stephen. "MacAllen says a minor one, thank God. She's talking. Her left arm's numb."

"Will she be all right?"

Stephen shrugged. "MacAllen says she's out of danger. No idea if she'll get the arm back. She's scared, I think. She'll want to see you."

The stairs creaked and groaned beneath their weight. It was as if the persistent winds off the sea had leached the very matter from the house. For a moment Colin imagined it like a blown-out egg shell, light enough to finally blow away in the wind.

The upstairs at least was more or less as Colin remembered. The furnishings and the inscrutable portraits of family ancestors were still here.

"Come on," Stephen said, turning away from their parents' room and toward his own. "I've got some decent clothes you can wear. You look ridiculous in that thing."

Colin followed him. He supposed a tuxedo was rather out of place here, especially after a chase across Nassau harbor and a night at sea. Stephen tossed him a pair of trousers and a shirt from his closet, and Colin quickly changed. Then Stephen led the way back down the hallway. He knocked once, then opened the door to his parents' bedroom. Colin followed him through, and there was his mother.

Emily Ridley looked frail, like the house and the farm. Time and unending struggle had changed her. Colin took in a breath as she looked up from the pillow, gray hair floating around her weathered face.

Doctor MacAllen was taking her pulse. "Colin," he said as he laid Emily's wrist down on the bedclothes. "She's had a stroke. I suppose Stephen told you. Minor impact to the left side. Numbness in the fingertips and forearm muscles, some loss of strength and reduced reflex response."

"Stop talking about me like a cadaver, Doctor," Emily said suddenly, "and let me greet my prodigal son. Come here, Colin, come here. You'll have to do most of the hugging, I'm afraid. This damned arm."

Colin grinned. There was the tough woman he'd known, the one who'd survived everything this island could throw at her and raised two rather troublesome sons into the bargain. He crossed the room as MacAllen helped her sit up, and he held her close.

"It's good to see you," he whispered.

"Well, you could have come anytime," Emily replied. "I've been right here."

"I know," he said. Of course, his mother knew that it wasn't that simple. Since the war, he'd been home a few times, but never for long. Too many elephants in the room. In the end, they always crowded him back out.

"What can be done for her?" he asked.

"Not much, really," said MacAllen. "She's not in danger right now. There's every hope for at least some recovery. Right now, she needs rest. In the longer term, a less strenuous lifestyle. You should retire to Nassau if you ask me, Emily."

"I didn't," she said. "And on what exactly am I to retire? I expect we'll have to pay you in chickens from the hen house."

"Well, let's not worry about that now," said MacAllen. "You two can talk for a few minutes, but not too much excitement. And then I want you to get some sleep."

"All right, all right," she sighed and patted the bedside with her good arm. "Now sit down and tell me all about Nassau."

STEPHEN STOOD AT THE SIDEBOARD, looking out across the flat, barren fields. Colin was still upstairs, happily chatting away with their mother about the glamorous life in Nassau. Stephen had left them to it. He poured himself a couple fingers of rum, then put the glass down untouched.

Colin always did this to him. The older brother, the dashing one, the charmer, the one who got away. Colin had gone off and joined the army when the war broke out, leaving him to keep the farm struggling along from season to season by the skin of his teeth. He'd been the one to try and keep the workers paid so they could feed their families. He'd been the one to take care of their mother as her health slowly failed her. It was too much to ask of him. It wasn't fair.

When the war finally ended, he thought Colin would return and help him. But he hadn't returned, or at least not for long. Colin had seen and done terrible things, so now he drank and gambled and caroused in Nassau. Well, things had been hard at home too, but he didn't have the luxury of running away. Colin had taken that.

He heard Colin coming down the stairs and quickly poured his drink back into its decanter.

"I think she'll sleep now," Colin said as he entered. "Did MacAllen have anything he didn't want to say in front of her?"

Stephen shook his head. "No. It's like he said. She'll pull through, but she needs to rest. She can't keep running the house the way she has."

Colin walked to the sideboard, and Stephen watched him pour himself the same drink he'd put back. Colin drained it in one long swallow. "Good stuff," he said, "this from Simon?"

"That's right."

Colin set the glass down with a heavy click and turned. "What's going on with the farm, Stephen? Why are the fields empty?"

Stephen felt a quick surge of anger. "Why? Because there's no goddamn money to plant them! That's why! Or pay the men. Why the hell do you think?"

"Could you pay them in shares? At least it would be something."

"Damn it, Colin, you don't know what the hell you're talking about. You haven't been here. I paid them in shares for the last two seasons. It wasn't enough. I owe most of them from a year ago. Market prices collapsed, and they're not coming back. Even if I could grow a real crop, I couldn't sell it."

Their father's initial success had been based on contracts to supply sisal fiber to the Royal Navy for use in rope. It had been a lucrative market once, but sail had long since given way to steam power. The Navy's demand for rope had plummeted, especially since the war ended. And what need there was could be met more cheaply by hemp fiber from Central and South America. The farm simply wasn't viable anymore.

"I didn't know it was that bad," said Colin. "I wasn't drawing my share, so I thought…"

"We couldn't have paid your share if you'd wanted it," said Stephen. "Not that you did anything to earn it."

Colin walked to the window and looked out at the barren fields. When he spoke, his voice was low and quiet.

"How are you getting by?"

Stephen scoffed. "We're not. Marcus, Peter, and a few of the others are still helping out, mostly because there's nothing else to do. We grow enough to trade a little. I'm growing some vegetables out back. There's some chickens. If mother needs care…what can you do?"

Colin turned back to him and his expression showed that he understood how hard that had been to ask. "Not a lot," he said softly. "I've got a nice boat and a sharp tuxedo. Enough to fit in with the rich tourists. But gambling's not what you'd call a reliable career. I live in a room over a bar."

The room fell silent. Colin poured himself another drink.

"So the problem, as I understand it," Colin said at last, "is that we need money, and fast."

Stephen smiled. "Very perceptive. That's most problems once you boil them down."

"Well," said Colin, "it happens I've been kicking around an idea in that vein."

"I'm listening."

"Those crazy Americans have gone and banned alcohol, haven't they?" Colin grinned. "And there's the Florida coast, just a hundred miles west. There's a land rush over there. High rollers are flooding in. They're buying lots sight unseen. They're building whole new towns overnight almost. Money's thick on the ground. And all that money makes people thirsty."

"You're joking. You want us to run booze into Florida?"

"All you need is a fast boat and some nerve. I've got the boat. *Pegasus* will outrun anything the Coast Guard's got. But I can't handle the cargo in Nassau. We'd need a base to operate from. Here. I can't do it alone, Stephen, but the two of us…"

Stephen put his face in one hand, then looked up in frustration. For a moment, he'd let himself think Colin had something to offer. "We're not criminals!"

"Well, we're not exactly landed gentry either, are we?" Colin shot back. "Father's plan didn't work out so well. It's time for a new one."

"And this is your idea? Become…outlaws?"

"For God's sake, I'm not talking about robbing people in the street!"

"This is so like you," Stephen said. "What happens to mother when we end up in prison? Or worse? Who's going to take care of her then?"

"We're going to take care of her. We're not going to prison. I know what I'm doing. I didn't just come up with this."

"You want to tell mother about this? What's she going to think?" Stephen's anger boiled over. It had been coming for a long time. "You don't get to do this. You don't get to charge in and act the hero with your half-witted…juvenile…you ran away,

Colin! You gave up your standing. And I understand the war was bad! I want to sympathize! But you left me to carry all this while you played 'lost generation' in your tuxedo with your stupid boat. And now we're supposed to fall in line so you can pose as a boot-legger to impress your tourist friends. That doesn't help me! I've got real problems here."

Colin's expression was dark, angry. He'd hit a sore spot. Good. He'd meant to. Colin moved toward him like a predator.

"What's your idea, then? Start a grocery store? Make shoes? We don't have a lot of options! I know how to fight, play cards, and race motorboats. You know how to run a farm into the ground. Not much money in either of those!"

"Hey!"

Emily's voice cut through the shouting, and the storm of emotion burst like a balloon. Instantly they were just two little boys, caught at something by their mother.

"MacAllen wants me to sleep," she said, tottering down the stairs.

Stephen rushed up to help her down. "Mother, be careful."

"I'm fine. Just cut out this arguing. Cut it out. I need you to hold each other up."

"Sorry, mother," said Colin.

Emily settled into a chair and swept her trembling right arm around the threadbare room. "Take a look. This is no time for false pride."

"You heard that?" Stephen asked.

"Hard not to."

"So what are you saying?"

"I'm saying what we all know. There's no future in this place. If there's a ready market for good rum in Florida, then don't worry about me holding my head up in polite society. I think you'll find money solves that problem too."

Stephen couldn't believe what he was hearing. "You...want us to..."

"From what I hear, it'll take you two working together," she said. "Just that would mean a lot to me. If you can make us rich into the bargain, I can live with my sons being criminals. Stupid law to begin with. Get me a shot of that rum over there, will you, Colin? It'll help me sleep. I'll need it if you two are going to keep waking me up like this."

Colin hurried to the sidebar and poured a small glass.

"We'll need more than a fast boat," Stephen said. "Where do we get starting money?"

Colin smiled as he handed Emily her drink. "It so happens, I've got an idea about that too."

3

It was two days later when Colin and Stephen set out for Nassau in an old cargo boat. Word that they had a plan to revive the farm spread quickly, but they tried to keep expectations low and didn't talk about the details. The idea was still half-formed. A lot of problems had to be overcome before they could put it into action.

They didn't say much on the crossing to New Providence Island. Long-simmering tensions had been brought to the surface over the last couple days. Neither brother wanted to hash those issues out here and now.

It was midday when they pulled into Nassau Harbor. The sun glittered off the water from a cloudless blue sky. The yachters' docks were studded with sails and the sleek hulls of steam yachts and motorboats. Colin checked the slip where *Camille* had been docked and saw it was empty. That was something at least. Hopefully Endicott had gone home to lick his wounds.

They made their way to the Harbormaster's office and sorted out the question of *Pegasus*. She'd been towed in as a hazard to navigation, and it took almost all the cash Colin had left to get her out of impound. But she was intact at least. They left the farm boat moored among the working boats and reclaimed *Pegasus*. Colin checked the engines and the fuel, happily surprised to find that nobody had siphoned the tanks dry before sending her into impound. She was ready for action. When he started up the Napier aircraft engine, its twelve cylinders gave off a reassuring purr, underlaid with a hint of snarl as if they were waiting for Colin to throw the throttle open and give the boat her head.

Colin smiled. *Not yet. But don't worry. You'll get to run soon enough.*

"Okay," he said, "Let's go see my friend Joe."

He steered east along the waterfront, toward old Fort Montagu. "Okay," he said over the purr of the engine, "let me tell you about Joe Gresham. She's a woman, first of all. She's got an awful lot of money, and she's kind of eccentric."

"Eccentric how?" Stephen asked.

"Just…eccentric."

"Okay."

"Just be polite," said Colin. "She's got money to burn. She can set us up for this. And she's a lot of fun once you get to know her. Good friend to have."

Colin kept *Pegasus* down to harbor speed and gave his brother the short briefing on Joe Gresham as they traveled. Her real name was Alice Barbara Gresham, and she came from big American oil money on her mother's side, but she was no society princess. At just sixteen, she'd joined the Red Cross and served as an ambulance driver during the war. When she got back, she'd started an all-female chauffeur service in London. She loved fast machines, especially racing boats, which was what had brought her to the Bahamas.

"And there's her shed," Colin said as he pulled up to a cluttered boatyard and cut the engines. From inside the shed, a hellish roar of engines shook the metal walls. Colin could feel it in his bones. An access channel ran into the shed so boats could be brought inside, but Colin brought *Pegasus* alongside a dock and they tied her off.

"Come on!" he shouted, and Stephen followed him inside.

The place was a boat mechanic's dream, packed with mahogany racing hulls, engines, and various esoteric parts. On one side of the access way, a sleek little hydroplane hull sat up on a rack with its engine removed. On the other, hanging from a bulky overhead crane, was a long racing boat. Its engines roared like thunder, shaking the boat and rattling the chains it hung from. Colin could see the exhaust stacks that rose from the stern shuddering and spitting smoke. He counted the stacks and realized the boat was powered by two W12s. *It must go like hell*, he thought. *Hope the hull can handle it.*

A few moments later the engines died down, their echoes gradually faded away, and relative quiet fell over the shed.

"It's no damn good," a voice said. "You need better shock mounts."

"Well, that's what we've got," said someone else.

"Hey, Joe!" Colin shouted.

Two grease-streaked faces popped up from the engineering compartment and looked down at them.

"Who...oh, hullo, Colin," one of them said. "Let's take a break, Roger."

The two of them climbed over the side of the boat and down a ladder. Colin grinned as Stephen tried not to gawk. Joe Gresham wore her hair cut short and slicked back with Brilliantine. A cigarette jutted from the corner of her mouth. She wore oil-stained coveralls with the sleeves rolled up to reveal a series of tattoos up her forearms.

She and Colin shook hands. "Been a while," she said. "You still fleecing those rich kids?"

"Got to get a new crop, I'm afraid. Played out that lot. Joe, meet my brother Stephen. Stephen, Joe Gresham."

"Pleasure," said Stephen as they shook hands.

Joe introduced her companion as Roger Carley. "That's his boat we're trying to whip into shape. There's a race in Montagu Bay tomorrow." She turned to Carley. "And my advice is to stay home. She's not ready."

"Well tomorrow's when the damn race is, Joe," Carley protested. "Nothing to do about that."

Joe shook her head and sighed. Then she noticed Stephen eyeing the hydroplane hull on the other side of the channel. "That one's mine," she said. "Doing some modifications to the power train. Not ready to run just yet, but she'll take the speed record when she is."

Stephen gestured to the name painted on the side of the hull. "Newg?"

Joe laughed. "Called her Gwen to begin with, after a girl-friend. First time I took her out for a trial run, the damn thing capsized on me. So they pull me out of the water and I'm looking at her, floating upside down there, and I said, 'all right then, damn you.' And since then she's been Newg."

Stephen laughed. "Well, put that way, it makes perfect sense."

Carley soon excused himself to check on some parts in the back of the shed. Joe tossed her cigarette butt into the channel and took another from a crumpled pack in a pocket of her coveralls.

"So what brings you boys around?" she asked.

"Business proposition," said Colin. Joe gave him a dubious look, and he quickly added, "the kind you'll like. There's a fast boat involved."

"Well that's all right, then," Joe laughed. "Maybe you better tell me about it."

They wandered outside and sat on the edge of the channel while Colin laid out his plan for running booze into the Florida coast.

"*Pegasus* is perfect for it," he said with a nod toward the boat, her polished mahogany hull gleaming in the sun. "She's got capacity, and she's fast. Nobody's going to run us down. There's plenty of supply, and we've got connections all up the coast ready to buy."

That last part was not entirely true. In fact, it was a bare-faced lie, but Colin expected finding buyers would be the easiest part of the operation. From what he'd heard in the casinos, they were practically lining up on the beach and waving lanterns for anyone who could get a steady supply of alcohol past the Coast Guard.

"All we need is a stake to get started," Colin concluded. "Enough to buy a cargo to run in. And the prices are premium. Double your money in no time. What do you say, Joe?"

He waited for an answer. He didn't like the look on Joe's face as she considered it.

"I like you, Colin," Joe said at last. That didn't sound good.

"You're fun to be around, you're a damn good card player. You've got a good, fast boat, and you know how to handle her. But I don't know about this."

"What's holding you back, if I may ask?" said Stephen.

Joe smiled. "Your brother's charming and fun," she told him, "and I've no doubt you're the same. But this is a criminal enterprise you're proposing. That's a matter of toughness and grit, and you don't strike me as a gangster, Colin. More than that, there's a hell of a risk involved. I don't want to get you into trouble you can't get out of. I don't want to see you have to dump a cargo and lose my money, or worse, end up in jail over there and it's my fault for putting you up to it."

She shook her head. "No, that settles it for me," she said. "I'm sorry, but the answer's no."

Colin took it in and said nothing. He knew there was nothing to gain by arguing with her. When Joe had made up her mind about something, it wasn't an easy matter to change it. She couldn't be argued with, but she could be impressed.

"Okay, Joe," he said after a few moments. "You've given us your reason, and that's fair. Thanks for listening."

They got up and Joe shook Colin's hand again. "Sorry to disappoint you," she said. "Good meeting you, Stephen. Good luck to both of you."

Then she nodded and headed back inside, shouting for Roger.

"Guess that didn't go like you expected, did it?" said Stephen as they walked back to *Pegasus*. "What are we going to do now? You got any other rich friends you can try?"

"No," said Colin, "she's the one."

"And she just turned us down flat," said Stephen. "So what do we do now?"

"We're going to show her she's wrong about us," said Colin.

"And how are we going to do that?"

They arrived back at *Pegasus*, and Colin bent down to untie her from the dock. He grinned and gestured at her.

"We're going to win a boat race."

4

As Colin had guessed, the race was an extremely informal affair. It was an officially unsanctioned exhibition put together by one of the big hotels to draw tourists. A number of serious speedboat racers happened to be spending the season in Nassau with an eye toward speed record runs. In addition to Joe and Roger Carley, Serra, the Italian daredevil, was in town. So were Guerin, the Frenchman from Corsica, and Sir Edgar Moresby, considered Britain's great hope to reclaim the Harmsworth Trophy from the seemingly unbeatable American, Gar Wood. Someone had noticed and put together the race to capitalize on their celebrity. The rest of the pack was local speedboat enthusiasts who'd turned up for a chance to say they'd raced against the world champions. Colin knew most of them, at least in passing.

As an exhibition, the usual tight restrictions on hull displacement and engine size had been dispensed with as well, which gave Colin and Stephen their opening. *Pegasus* was designed by generalists. She didn't quite fit any of the cup classes. But just a day before the race, they had no problem entering her.

Colin spent much of the evening preparing Stephen to serve as engineer. They tuned the powerful aircraft engine, flushed the fuel lines, adjusted control linkages, and generally did all they could to get themselves and the boat ready.

"This is fine," Stephen said at one point. "But if these boats we're up against are meant to set world records, how are we going to win?"

"Those boats are thoroughbreds," said Colin. "Everything that doesn't make it go faster comes out. So they're fast, but they can't take any punishment. We're going to outlast them."

Stephen looked dubious. "They're not even going to finish? Surely they can't be that flimsy. What would be the point?"

Colin adjusted a valve on the engine until he was satisfied. "You saw Carley's boat, right? Twin engines, twenty-four cylinders. She's got power all right. Too much power. And he'll push it too hard trying to win. They all do. They push until something breaks. They lose drive shafts, oil lines."

"So your plan is for everyone faster than us to drop out of the race before the finish?" Stephen laughed. "That's dicey, even for you!"

Colin shrugged. "Best I could come up with on short notice. And maybe we can impress Joe even if we don't win."

Stephen shook his head, and they got back to work.

RAIN BLEW THROUGH OVERNIGHT, but it cleared by late morning. By race time, the sun gleamed brightly off the waters of Montagu Bay, but there was still a bit of wind and a choppy surface. It was no problem for *Pegasus*, but Colin thought it would slow down the pack.

In the morning, Colin and Stephen attended the pre-race briefing on rules and safety. Then the crews walked out to their boats, all in off-white coveralls, helmets and goggles. Eleven boats formed up at the start. They were a motley bunch. The big names had refined racing boats with custom-built hulls and specialized engines. The local crowd drove stock boats they'd tuned as best they could. *Pegasus* occupied a spot somewhere in the middle with her Gar Wood hull and modified airplane engine. She was a respectable racer and would probably be the boat to beat in any race that didn't include so many trophy winners. Carley was at the head of the pack among the other serious contenders. As Colin expected, he'd ignored Joe's advice and come out to race.

"You really think we can do this?" Stephen shouted over the roar of engines.

"Little late to back out now," Colin shouted back. "Just watch the oil pressure. We'll be pushing her pretty hard."

"I thought that's why those guys aren't going to finish."

Colin patted the hull affectionately. "She'll take it," he said. "Besides, those are one-man boats. They'll be doing it all themselves. We've got an engineer! You're our secret weapon, Stephen!"

Stephen scoffed. "Extra weight, you mean."

"You'll do fine."

The course was laid out in a long triangle of buoys. There would be three laps, enough to excite the crowd on the shore, but not long enough for them to get bored.

The marshal's boat took up position in the center of the triangle, and the rescue boats moved to their positions. Colin listened to the bursts of power as the racers gunned their engines.

Then the marshal fired a starting flare, and the bay erupted into spray, exhaust, and bone-shaking noise. Colin threw the throttle open, and *Pegasus* lurched into the fray.

The pack quickly spread out more or less as Colin expected. Guerin, Carley, Serra, and Moresby quickly shot into the lead with the other boats strung out in a line behind them. One of the locals had gotten a particularly good start and *Pegasus* was running behind him, but by the first turn they were bearing down on him.

And the turn was decisive. Colin cut inside and deftly steered tight around the buoy. The other boat had the speed to match *Pegasus* in a straight run but couldn't keep up with her in the turns. By the time the other boat cleared the turn, *Pegasus* was well ahead and accelerating down the back stretch.

Colin smiled at Stephen, but Stephen wasn't looking at him. He was looking straight ahead with an expression of raw joy.

Colin grinned and turned his attention back to the boats ahead. Serra and Carley were fighting for the lead with Guerin close behind. Moresby was well back in fourth. Then there was a long stretch of empty water, and then *Pegasus*. If he could overtake even one of those boats ahead of him, that would be something worth talking about. Even if Joe didn't change her mind about backing them, placing well here would open doors.

Now they just had to do it.

Little changed through the first lap. There was some jockeying among the leaders, and a lot of it in the back of the pack. But the leaders were still the leaders, the also-rans were still also running, and *Pegasus* was stuck somewhere in the middle.

Then, partway into lap two, a cloud of dark smoke erupted ahead of them. *Pegasus* shot into it, and Colin's goggles were spattered with oil.

"What's that?" Stephen shouted. "What happened?"

Colin furiously wiped his goggles and peered through the smoke. There was a boat in trouble just ahead. He made out a looming shape veering across his path and steered to avoid it.

"It's Guerin!" he shouted to Stephen. "Blew an oil line. He's out!"

Then they shot out of the cloud, and visibility returned. Guerin limped toward shore behind them, trailing smoke. Ahead of them, Serra and Carley were neck and neck in the lead, and... Colin slapped Stephen's shoulder and pointed ahead. They were gaining on Moresby.

"How are we doing that?" Stephen shouted.

There was no obvious trouble, but Moresby was losing speed. Colin pushed the Lion's gauges to the red line, and they continued to close on him. Then, somehow, impossibly, they were abreast of him. Colin glanced over and saw Moresby bending over in the cockpit, furiously adjusting something below Colin's line of sight. And then they were past him and into third place.

Colin didn't have time to celebrate. The second turn was coming up fast. He whipped the boat around the buoy and accelerated down the straight. Then he whooped and slapped Stephen's back. Just two more to catch.

Of course, that wasn't likely. Serra and Carley were well ahead, fighting for the lead. Serra had it at the moment, but Carley was pushing hard, driving his boat through the chop with his engines screaming.

Colin glanced back and saw Moresby gaining on them again. He must have fixed whatever wasn't right. Colin wondered if he could hold on for another lap.

Then Carley's boat simply disintegrated. One moment he was approaching the third turn. The next, there was nothing but a cloud of wooden fragments tearing up the surface of the bay at nearly a hundred miles an hour. Serra wrapped around the buoy and blasted away down the straight.

Colin didn't hesitate. He cut the throttle and steered toward the wreck.

"Emergency kit!" he shouted at Stephen, gesturing to the locker beneath the seat. Then he brought *Pegasus* to a stop, surrounded by floating fragments of Carley's hull. He made out a larger shape beneath the surface.

"What are you doing?" Stephen shouted, but Colin didn't answer. He tore off his helmet and dove over the side. The warm waters of the bay closed over him.

Instantly the roar of engines became a muted, distant drone. Below him, a large chunk of the boat spiraled slowly down toward the bottom of the bay. He saw an arm waving in the current as it turned.

Colin swam down with strong, steady strokes. As he approached, the chunk of debris spun and revealed Carley. He was unconscious, strapped into his seat. A thin stream of blood spiraled up from his forehead. The piece of debris he was strapped to included the cockpit floor, and perhaps six feet of gunwale. Colin caught up with it and pulled at the straps securing Carley to the seat. There was a complicated metal latch that seemed to have jammed. The straps were tight, leaving no room to pull Carley free.

He needed air, and soon. No time. Colin grabbed the chunk of wood with both arms and kicked his way toward the surface. He rose slowly, fighting the drag of the heavy wood and Carley's body. The surface seemed to glimmer just out of reach as his lungs burned and his body told him to breathe. *Breathe!*

Finally he broke the surface and took a deep, gasping breath. Still unconscious, Carley shuddered and vomited water. Colin felt the weight dragging him down again and knew he couldn't stay above water for long. Stephen was reaching frantically for him.

"Knife!" Colin shouted. "Knife!"

The water closed over him once again and the wreckage pulled him toward the bottom. A moment later, there was a splash and the heavy utility knife from *Pegasus'* toolbox tumbled slowly down through the water.

Colin desperately reached for it. The first time he fumbled it off his fingertips and felt a rush of horror as it spun away through the darkening water. He lunged for it once more and this time caught the hilt between two fingers. He pulled the knife in and furiously slashed at Carley's straps.

Finally, he pulled Carley free and let the huge chunk of shattered wood fall away. It spiraled down into the murk as Colin grasped Carley to his chest and kicked desperately for the light above.

When he broke the surface, he took a grateful breath and looked for *Pegasus*. He saw Stephen waving frantically at him from the cockpit. He was shouting something, but Colin couldn't hear a thing. He felt more than heard the rush of the approaching boat. A dark shape bore down on him, fast and huge.

In panic, Colin dove and swam down, dragging Carley behind him. Above him, the boat blew past him like a freight train. The wake sent him tumbling through the water, and he nearly lost his grip on Carley. He swam for light, gasping and disoriented.

He dragged Carley's head above water and backstroked toward *Pegasus*. He felt Stephen grab his wrist, and together they helped haul the inert form of Roger Carley over the side. Then, finally, Colin saw the race rescue boat approaching.

THE VICTORY STAND was a wooden platform in front of the grandstands. The awards ceremony was already underway as *Pegasus* coasted up to the dock alongside the other racers. They'd handed Carley over to the crew of the rescue boat, who had hurried him off to Nassau's hospital.

On the way in, Stephen had explained what had happened. On the final lap, Serra and Moresby, the two remaining professionals, had traded the lead more than once. Moresby was ahead as they approached the wreck and *Pegasus*. Moresby had gone wide to give them plenty of room. But Serra had cut inside, as close to the buoy as he could. In the process he'd passed no more than ten feet from *Pegasus* and very nearly run Colin down.

It had worked. Serra had retaken the lead and held it to be first across the finish line.

Stephen fumed as they walked up the dock. A local dignitary held the trophy while he made his speech. Serra stood beside him, beaming, waiting for his prize. The other racers looked on in a line along the platform.

"Son of a bitch almost killed you," Stephen muttered. "For what? You said this isn't even a real race!"

"Calm down," said Colin, though he didn't feel very calm himself. The official finished his speech, and there was some uninspired applause as he handed Serra the cup.

"Like hell, I will!" Stephen snapped. He charged down the platform, past the startled competitors. Serra turned at the commotion, and Stephen threw a right cross that caught him on the chin and threw him back. The cup flew off the platform and tumbled to the beach below.

"That was my brother you almost ran down, you jackass!" Stephen shouted as Serra lay the platform. "Get up!"

Racers and hotel officials converged and hauled Stephen back. Serra stood up, shouting in Italian and gesturing. More men held him back. Colin heard Guerin tell Serra, "It's done. You earned that, *connard*."

The crowd certainly seemed to approve. Stephen drew considerably more applause than Serra himself had. Colin took his arm and pulled him toward the dock. Behind them, the crowd jeered Serra as someone went to retrieve his trophy.

"Thanks," Colin said. "But I can fight my own fights."

Stephen grinned. "Sure you can. That was for me. You want to go back and knock him down yourself, be my guest."

Colin smiled. They walked down the beach until the ceremony was well out of sight. Then they headed into the working part of town and grabbed drinks at a fishermen's bar. Finally, they decided they should go retrieve *Pegasus*.

Outside the hotel they ran into Joe Gresham holding court with a group of dandies that Colin didn't recognize. She wore a tailored suit and punctuated her statements with a cigar in one hand. When she spotted them she excused herself and crossed the street, waving her cigar.

"There you two are!" she said. "Wondered where you got to. You got a good right there," she added to Stephen.

"Any word on Roger?" Colin asked.

"He'll make it," said Joe. "Broke his wrist, couple of ribs. He won't be driving for a while. But he'll live, and that's thanks to you two."

Colin nodded. "Couldn't just leave him."

Joe looked around then drew them both closer. "You weren't lying," she said. "That's a fast boat. And you've got some balls on you too. If you're still looking to run rum into Florida, I'll stake you."

5

COLIN AND STEPHEN RETURNED TO BECKERS CAY THE NEXT morning. Emily was doing well. The strength in her arm was returning, though she was still weaker than before the stroke. Doctor MacAllen had come by the previous day and approved of her progress. He couldn't promise her strength would fully return, but he said he was hopeful.

Colin wandered through the fields, reacquainting himself with the land. He'd have been a poor choice to take over from their father, he knew. Things would have gone much worse if he'd stayed to run the farm and Stephen had gone to the army. He was certain of that. He couldn't have done any better here than Stephen had, and Stephen wasn't cut out for war. Colin had seen plenty of young men arrive at the front who reminded him of his younger brother. They were all full of fire and pride, eager to prove themselves, and they were all dead now.

No, better the way it worked out, he told himself as he walked back to the house. They were both here. Colin had a fast boat and a bundle of Joe Gresham's cash in his satchel upstairs. They could leave the past behind and make their own future.

"You two be careful out there," Emily said over an early

dinner. The sun was still high in the window of the threadbare dining room. "And for God's sake, remember you're brothers. You're going to sea and you're breaking the law. There'll be no room for your squabbling."

After dinner, they collected their gear. Emily kissed them both one last time. 'Don't linger,' she said.

Colin smiled. "Make our run and right home. We won't make you worry."

"Okay then," said Emily. "Off with you."

Then they left the house behind and walked down the trail to the dock. Colin took a last look over *Pegasus*. The tanks were full, the engine was tuned and ready. He patted the thin bundles of cash in special pockets he'd sewn into the lining of his windbreaker.

"Let's do it," he said.

Stephen cast off and stepped aboard. Colin started the engine and let it race. He could almost feel the boat straining forward, eager to run. He patted the wheel. Soon enough. For now, he cruised away from the dock at a comfortable speed and steered west.

THE WEATHER WAS CLEAR, the sea calm, and the crossing uneventful. The sun glowed a soft red near the horizon when Colin spotted a plume of smoke in the distance.

"There," he said, pointing it out to Stephen.

"We're there already?" Stephen said in surprise.

"That's it. The rum line. Twelve miles out. Past there, we're in American waters. That's where we step outside the law."

As they drew closer, a rough shape on the water gradually resolved into a cluster of ships. Around them was a flotilla of smaller boats. There were fishing boats, speedboats, at least one example of almost anything seaworthy, it seemed. They rode alongside the larger ships or fluttered from one to the next. Ship's dinghies served as water taxis. Colin slowed to a harbor pace and pulled in past a grimy Mexican freighter.

"It's like a small town out here!" said Stephen.

"A wild west town. They bring big loads in and park here, where the Coast Guard can't touch them. Then they wait. Sell off the cargo to runners a piece at a time until they're out."

"How long does that take?"

Colin shrugged. "Depends, I guess. Most of these small boats are likely headed for Miami. Plenty of market there. I don't guess it would take them too long to drink these ships dry."

A female voice shouted down from another freighter as they passed. "Hey handsome, nice boat."

Colin glanced up. She was tall, sleek, and beautiful. She wore a beaded drop-waist dress, and her black hair was cropped short.

"Why don't you come up and buy me a drink, you charmer?" she called down at them. Colin just smiled and waved.

"No law, sailors, time to kill, and plenty of booze," said Stephen. "I guess there's more to do out here than just buy a cargo."

They found a likely looking ship, the *General Matorras*, flying the Chilean flag. She had a floating dock alongside, so they pulled up. A waiting sailor caught their rope and tied them off. Then they headed up the metal stairs to the main deck.

There was a party on deck. Colored lights had been strung along the superstructure, and Colin heard a piano thumping out a jazz tune from below decks. Couples danced or simply made out against the ship's railings. The women seemed far better dressed and groomed than their companions.

An officer waited at the top of the stairs. "Welcome aboard, gentlemen," he said as they stepped onto the deck. "If you're here to buy, we have much to offer, from gin and vodka to the finest French champagnes."

"We're here to buy," he said.

The officer smiled. "Then please enjoy yourselves below decks."

A door at the back of the forecastle led them below. The music was louder here, drifting up from the holds. They pressed their backs against the bulkhead as a laughing woman led a very drunk boatman down the corridor toward the cabins. Then they headed down.

The freighter's main cargo hold had been converted into a surprisingly credible nightclub. There were tables and chairs, a long wooden bar, and a dance floor. The furniture didn't match, and the back wall behind the bar was made of stacked wooden crates. But Colin had been in worse clubs on land.

The piano player banged out a dance tune on a battered upright in the corner. Lights strung from the ceiling cast odd shadows as people moved. Smoke drifted overhead in lazy clouds.

"Okay," Stephen murmured, "now what?"

Colin looked over the bar. He spotted several tables where deals appeared to be going down. So it wasn't just the ship's crew selling off their own cargo. Other runners were acting as brokers for them, or perhaps buying from the ship and then flipping the cargo for a profit. Colin noted a man eyeing them from a shadowy table in the corner opposite the piano. He looked like a likely prospect.

"Go to the bar and keep your eyes open," Colin murmured. "I'm going to go talk to a man about some booze."

STEPHEN FOUND an empty stool and sat at the bar. He ordered a shot of whiskey and watched the room, trying to figure the place out. There was the bartender, kept busy by a pair of women who brought back orders and delivered drinks to tables. There was the piano player in the corner, seemingly oblivious to everything but his keyboard. Who ran this place? Where were the rest of the crew?

There, he thought, his eye landing on a table near the dance floor. One man sat there alone. He held a shot glass in one hand, but he didn't drink from it. Instead he seemed to be watching the flow of conversation, turning at a loud voice and checking the door as newcomers arrived.

A guard, Stephen thought. *That'll be a pistol under his jacket there. Here to keep the peace.* It seemed like a good idea. The crowd wasn't exactly drawn from Burke's Peerage. It looked like a place where a fight might break out at any moment. The wild west indeed.

He glanced over at Colin, sitting with the mysterious man in the corner. The two of them leaned close in intense conversation.

"You buying or selling?" said a voice at his side.

Stephen looked back in surprise. The man was tall and rangy, with brown hair and a sparkle in his blue eyes. One hand idly moved a half-full shot glass back and forth around on the bar.

"Buying," he said. "You selling?"

"No," the man replied, "I'm waiting. Had some trouble with the boat. My partner's taken her ashore to deal with it, and I'm keeping an eye on the cargo out here. Name's Blake. Sam Blake."

Blake offered a meaty hand, and they shook.

"Stephen Ridley."

"You a limey, Stephen? I mean from that accent."

"Bahamas," said Stephen with a laugh. "Close enough."

"Well then, let me buy you a drink in the spirit of international cooperation." Blake waved at the bartender. *"Uno mas! Para mi y mi amigo!"* Then he turned to Stephen and said conspiratorially, "Don't worry, they all speak English. Figure if I'm going to be here a few days, best make a good impression."

The bartender poured them a pair of shots. Blake raised his. "To the Volstead Act," he said, "God bless it!"

They downed their drinks, and Stephen found himself barely

able to breathe. He struggled to keep from coughing, and it was a few moments before he could speak.

"Good God, what is that?" he asked when he could.

Blake laughed. "That's pisco, my friend. From Chile. They drink it like water down there. They've got a ton of it aboard, and turns out nobody much wants it up here. So it's cheap at the bar."

Stephen shuddered. "They could clean rust off the hull with it!"

Blake laughed. "Starting to develop a taste for the stuff myself. Been here more than a week now. I haven't seen you and your partner before. You new in town?"

"My brother, Colin," Stephen said. "And you're right. First time here."

"Well, if you want to run into Florida, I hope you've got a fast boat. Coast Guard's cracking down. Deployed a brand new cutter out here, the *Mojave*. She's been picking off runners left and right."

Stephen grinned. "I don't think she'll catch *Pegasus*."

"Better be sure," said Blake. "Word is she's got five-inch deck guns, a brace of machine guns, and she'll do fifteen knots. Not something you want to tangle with."

"Fifteen knots?" Stephen laughed. "Won't be a problem."

"Hope you're right. Another one?"

Stephen nodded. "My turn. Maybe they've got some gin?"

Blake laughed. "They've got whatever you want."

Stephen waved for the bartender.

"So where you want to take your cargo once you've got one?" Blake asked.

"Haven't decided," said Stephen. "How about you? Once your partner gets back?"

"Miami," said Blake. "Good money to be made, but I wouldn't start out there fresh. Most of the Miami business is sewn up. Big loads going in, kind that bribe their way in 'cause they're too big to sneak in. Only reason I can work it is because my partner's got the connections."

Blake downed his gin. "Much appreciated. Now, if you're in a smaller speedboat—what, about thirty feet probably? Big enough to haul a load, but still fast?"

Stephen shrugged.

"Yeah, I'd go north of Miami. Smaller towns up there. Find the right place, you can make some dough." An idea occurred to him. "You know, you might try Harmony Beach."

"Where's that?"

"New place," said Blake. "Not surprised you haven't heard of it. Little vacation town. They're springing up all down the coast. The place you're looking for is the Harmony Beach Motorboat Club. I hear they're looking for a steady supplier. Their last runner got picked off by the Coast Guard. But a fast thirty-footer like your *Pegasus*? Well, I'm sure you won't have any trouble."

"Why are you telling me this?" Stephen asked. "You could take their business for yourself."

Blake laughed. "Not without a boat, I can't! "He slapped the surface of the bar. "Besides, you see this bar here? When I got here, it was about eight feet farther out! They run out of booze, they just take down another row of crates and make the dance floor a little bigger. And there's half a dozen ships just like this one out here at any one time. Hell, Steve, can I call you Steve? There's an endless supply of booze out here, and an endless supply of customers ready to pay for it. No need to be greedy!"

Stephen conceded the point with a nod. Maybe this really was going to be as easy as Colin thought. If it was easy to buy here and easy to sell on the Florida coast, then all they had to worry about was the Coast Guard in the middle. And if they couldn't do better than fifteen knots, they deserved to get caught.

"Of course, I guess not everyone sees it that way," Blake said suddenly, nodding over Stephen's shoulder. Stephen turned to see a newcomer, slightly wobbly, looking around with a bitter, angry glare.

"Scogins," said Blake. "Keep your distance from that one. He drinks up more of a load than he gets ashore. And he's a mean bastard too. Unpredictable."

The newcomer, Scogins, stalked toward the table where Colin sat. Colin passed a sheaf of bills across the table, and the other man quickly folded them and stuck them inside his coat. Then Scogins arrived, standing off to Colin's side, and they traded words. At first, Stephen couldn't make them out, but the voices quickly rose.

"You had no right!" Scogins barked at the other man. "We had a deal. That was my cargo."

"Not until you pay for it!" the man behind the table answered angrily. "You know the terms. No cash, no delivery. Load's sold now."

Stephen could see this was not going to end well. "Excuse me," he said to Blake and stood up from the barstool.

"That's my load!" Scogins shouted, loud enough now that heads were turning across the bar.

Stephen put his hand in the pocket of his windbreaker and started toward the table. He hadn't gotten more than two steps before Colin stood up.

"Look around, friend," said Colin, "there's plenty more where that came from."

Scogins turned on Colin. "Play me for a sucker? That what you think?" He lashed out suddenly and hit Colin's shoulder. Colin wasn't ready for the blow and spun. He nearly fell before he caught himself on the table.

In an instant, Scogins whipped out a long, wicked-looking blade and pressed it to Colin's throat. Colin froze.

"Who's the big man now?" Scogins shouted. "My cargo! Put it on my boat!"

Stephen strode quickly up behind Scogins. He pulled a Colt

Hammerless automatic pistol from his pocket and jammed the muzzle against the back of Scogins' skull.

"You so much as twitch, and after this place closes, they'll be mopping up your brains along with the vomit."

Scogins didn't move, but suddenly there were guns everywhere. The bartender, the guard Stephen had spotted earlier, and another one he hadn't. Even the piano player was standing with a cut down rifle leveled at them.

"That's enough!" the guard snapped. "Drop 'em now. All of them."

"He goes first," Stephen said, standing still with the Colt in his outstretched arm.

"Okay," said Scogins. "Okay, okay."

Scogins removed the knife from Colin's throat and placed it on the table. Then Stephen slowly lowered the pistol and put it back in his pocket. A guard quickly confiscated the knife and led Scogins out of the hold. The tension gradually faded, and conversations resumed. The piano player sat back down and picked up his tune right where he'd left off.

"You didn't tell me you had that," said Colin as they walked back to the bar.

"Thought I might find a use for it," said Stephen. "Better prepared than sorry."

Colin didn't answer. As they approached the bar, the bartender gave them a look. Blake got off his stool and wobbled slightly.

"Well, you two are good for a bit of excitement anyway," he said. "By the way, you're still here because that wasn't your fault. But they don't care for people waving guns around in the middle of their operation."

"We're just leaving," said Colin, "Mr.?"

Stephen introduced them, and they shook. "Probably a good idea to head out," said Blake. "Now that you've got your cargo. Was just telling your brother here, you might want to try

Harmony Beach. About two eighty degrees and straight on to the shore. Look for the Harmony Beach Motorboat Club and ask for Melissa."

Colin thanked him and nudged Stephen. "Let's pick up our load and get moving. We're not making any money here."

6

It was dark by the time *Pegasus* was refueled and ready to go. The forward passenger cockpit and cargo bay were loaded with gin. The bottles were packed in burlocks, burlap bags full of straw. Each one took three bottles on the bottom, two more upside down on top of them, and one more right side up on top of those. Then the bag was stitched shut. They were a rumrunner invention, Colin explained. They let a boat carry three times the cargo it could carry in bulky wooden crates. What's more, they were easier to handle in a small boat getting rocked by the waves, and they caused less breakage than crates.

"Where'd you learn all this?" Stephen asked as they packed the last few burlocks onto the front passenger seats.

Colin grinned. "Hanging around unsavory characters in bars. Very educational."

Then they cast off, fired up the Lion engine, and steered away into the night.

"Checked the charts," Colin shouted over the engine as the lights of the Rum Line fell away behind them. "Harmony Beach is where he says it is all right. Doesn't look like there's much there, though."

"Why would he send us on a wild goose chase?" Stephen shouted back. "What's in it for him?"

"No idea. We'll check it out, I guess. If there's nothing there, we can just go up the coast a bit. Plenty of thirsty towns."

Stephen nodded, and Colin hoped he was right. He didn't want to admit it, but he didn't know nearly as much about bootlegging as he'd led Stephen, their mother, and Joe to believe. But he knew people who were making big money doing this, and they weren't as smart as he was. He could do this.

The sea was calm, the night was quiet, and they made good time. Colin maintained a steady heading and kept his eyes out for trouble.

He spotted it before Stephen did.

Suddenly, Colin cut the engine and slapped the switches that turned off *Pegasus'* running lights. The boat rocked gently.

"What's going on?" said Stephen.

Colin pointed off to the port quarter. "There."

In the distance were ship's lights, moving in their direction.

"Is it the Coast Guard?" Stephen asked nervously.

"Probably," said Colin. Then a spotlight flashed bright in the darkness and began sweeping the water ahead of the ship. "Definitely."

"They know we're here!"

"Looks that way." *Pegasus* had been running with her lights on, and the sound of her engine would carry a long way over these calm seas. From the movement of the light, it looked like the ship was heading straight toward them.

"Time to move," said Colin. He left the lights off but turned the engine back on at low rpms and steered off into the darkness at an angle.

Almost immediately a voice boomed over the water from an amplified horn. "Unidentified vessel, this is the Coast Guard Cutter *Mojave*. Heave to, turn on your lights, and stand by for inspection."

"Yeah," Colin muttered, "not going to do that."

He spun the wheel, zigzagging at quarter speed to confuse them. Then he shut the engine down again, and *Pegasus* drifted silently with the gentle waves.

"Can't we just outrun them?" Stephen murmured.

"I don't want them to open fire on us." The Coast Guard had been known to do that to force a boat to stand down.

"Let's just lay low for now," said Colin, "and see if they give up."

The cutter hadn't been able to follow them in the dark. They were searching on the wrong heading, sweeping their searchlight over empty sea. But he didn't know how long they would keep searching. Colin and Stephen sat in silence, barely breathing. They listened and watched the cutter's lights as it turned back toward them.

"They'll find us," Stephen whispered.

"Then we'll run."

"Wait. You hear that?"

Colin listened. He did hear something. It sounded like another engine in the distance. How far away he couldn't tell. But the *Mojave's* crew had heard it too. They watched as the cutter wheeled around, her stacks spitting smoke into the night sky. The searchlight swept past them, and the cutter raced away at top speed.

"Someone did us a good turn," Colin said. "So many runners out here they don't know who they're chasing."

The *Mojave* was headed away from them now, chasing the new boat. "Let's return the favor," said Colin. He brought the engine back up to full speed with a defiant roar, and the *Pegasus* raced away toward the Florida coast in the distance.

"Are they turning back for us?" Colin shouted.

"No," Stephen answered. "Sticking with the other boat."

Colin shrugged. Then he laughed and couldn't stop. He looked over and saw Stephen laughing as well, and he slapped him on the shoulder. They'd dodged a heavily armed Coast Guard cutter! They'd slipped through the perimeter with their illicit cargo and were headed safely for Florida and payday. They'd done it!

Stephen took the knife from the toolbox and sliced open a burlock he'd claimed from the cargo. He took out a bottle of gin, opened it, and raised it to the stars. Then he took a swallow and handed the bottle to Colin.

"This stuff's terrible!" he shouted as Colin took a swig. Colin had to agree.

"They've cut it with something," Stephen announced.

"Sure tastes that way," said Colin. "And you know the best part? We get it there, nobody's going to care!"

He tossed the bottle over the side, and *Pegasus* powered on toward the distant lights of Florida.

HARMONY BEACH WAS on a barrier island. A narrow channel separated it from the mainland, part of the new Intracoastal Waterway that ran all the way down the coast. At either end of the island were gaps carved by the sea. Colin steered for the northern gap because he saw more lights there. As they passed, they saw a small fleet of docked boats and a cluster of brightly-lit buildings. Music drifted across the water as they moved slowly past at harbor speed.

"That looks like it," said Colin. He scanned the docks and the structures. Now that they were here, he wasn't entirely sure how to approach the place. He felt a fluttering rhythm in his heart knowing *Pegasus* was loaded down with a cargo that could land them both in jail.

"How do we go in?" Stephen asked. Apparently, he was having the same concerns.

"Sounds like they're having a hell of a party over there," Colin observed. "Never saw a party like that without plenty of booze. But yeah, we should be careful."

He gunned the throttle slightly and headed past the club. Farther down the island, the lights quickly thinned out into darkness. And unlike the bare beach on the ocean side, the channel side of the island was thick with foliage and mangrove clusters.

"Look for a place we can slip in and hide the boat," he told Stephen. "We'll go in on foot and see what's what."

They took the boat in as close to shore as they could and glided slowly past the trees. Colin watched ahead for sandbars or logs in the water, while Stephen scanned the shore. It was slow going in the dark.

"There," Stephen said after a few minutes. He pointed out an inlet shrouded by overhanging branches. Colin could only see it at all because of the way the moonlight glinted off the water beyond the shoreline.

Colin cut the engine and pulled a couple wooden poles from a space along the side of the hull. He handed one to Stephen. Then they took up positions on opposite sides and pushed the boat in toward shore. *Pegasus* disappeared beneath the branches. About thirty feet in, she ground gently against the sandy bottom.

"Perfect," Colin announced. He couldn't see any lights at all. He heard only night sounds. There were two trees nearby to tie off the boat, and a gentle rise beyond them that would get them out of the water.

"We should take a sample, shouldn't we?" Stephen asked as they were tying the boat up.

"Good idea."

Colin produced a hip flask and filled it from one of the bottles in the burlock they'd opened. He considered it, then shrugged and slipped it into his pocket. "Let's hope they're thirsty."

Fifteen minutes later, they were walking up the island's main road. It was a narrow belt of asphalt flanked by sand, scattered clumps of sea grass, and wooden stakes marking out lots for planned construction. From time to time, they'd pass a sign promising, "Coming soon, another fine home from Kusack Florida Properties."

"Quite the holiday paradise," Stephen observed.

Colin chuckled. "If stakes were mansions, this would be the Riviera."

Headlights appeared behind them, and they stepped off the pavement as a car blew past. The driver thrust out a feminine arm and shouted something Colin couldn't quite make out. The car went weaving down the road, taillights fading into the darkness.

They reached a few actual houses as they approached the north end of the island, and a battered sign welcomed them to the town of Harmony Beach. Beyond the distinctly modest houses were a few small stores, dark and quiet now. Nothing moved as they walked through town. It didn't take them long.

On the far side of the small cluster of houses, the road went on another few hundred yards and ended at the entrance to the Harmony Beach Motorboat Club. Even from a distance, Colin could tell it was probably worth more than the rest of Harmony Beach put together—discounting the prime real estate, of course.

They walked through a parking lot full of coupes and touring cars, with a speedster or two for good measure. Beyond that, a walkway led up to the front doors where a pair of large men in suits watched them coming.

"Who are we here to see again?" Colin murmured.

"Melissa."

They stopped at the doors. The bouncers looked them over without smiling, and one said, "Can I help you gentlemen?"

"We're here to see Melissa," said Colin.

The other bouncer reached over and pulled open the door.

"Welcome to the Harmony Beach Motorboat Club," he said. His intonation sounded like he'd practiced the line in front of a mirror. "Have a good time."

Colin thanked them, and they went inside.

7

"That was easier than I thought," Stephen said as the doors closed behind them. The place smelled of cigarette smoke, and the noise hit him like the blast from an oven. "They don't seem too worried about the cops."

Colin smiled. "Doesn't look that way, does it? I was expecting a door with a little barred window and a gangster to grill us before he let us in."

They left their coats with a check girl in the vestibule and headed inside. Stephen let his eyes adjust to the brightness and soaked in the ambience. The decor was meant to be nautical, but it struck Stephen as what someone might think of who'd only read about boats. There were fishing nets strung along the walls, whaling harpoons, brass propellers. A large stuffed tarpon hung from the ceiling. It was a mishmash of anything remotely related to the water.

But nobody seemed interested in the furnishings. A raucous dance band played on a stage at the far end of the hall. Couples danced in the center, the women in beaded flapper dresses and the men mostly in suits. Stephen felt underdressed suddenly, but

55

as he looked around he saw other men dressed with less polish. They sat and drank, alone or in pairs, at tables around three sides of the dance floor. The bar took up the fourth side.

A waiter headed their way, a full tray balanced on his arm. He veered toward them. "Get you something, gentlemen?"

"Thank you, we'll go to the bar," said Stephen. "Can we find Melissa there?"

"Frank's the bartender," said the waiter. "If she's not there, he can set you up."

Then he was gone, and they headed through the packed tables toward the bar.

"Where do all these people live?" Stephen asked. "They sure didn't all come from that ghost town outside."

"Along the coast, I guess," said Colin. "Place like this might pull customers from the mainland for miles both ways. Plenty of boats outside. And those cars. There must be a bridge over the channel somewhere."

They found a narrow open space at the bar, and Colin caught the bartender's attention. He was a thin man with unruly black hair and an anchor tattoo on his forearm.

Colin beckoned him closer.

"What can I get you?" the bartender asked with a smile. "It's slim pickings tonight, I'm afraid. No gin, no rum. Some rye, but if that's your drink I'd order a double while we've got it."

"You Frank?" Colin asked.

"That's right."

"Colin Ridley. My brother Stephen. We're looking for Melissa."

Frank's eyes narrowed slightly. "Yeah? Why's that?"

Stephen looked around at the patrons knocking back drinks as fast as they could get them. If there was anywhere safe to reveal their purpose...

"I think we might be able to help with your gin problem," Colin said.

"Do tell. Well, enjoy a couple shots on me, and I'll track her down."

Frank produced a bottle of whiskey and poured them two shots. They slid across the bar with a grating sound. Then Frank headed down the bar and leaned close to speak to another man.

"Now we wait," said Colin, and he raised his glass.

Stephen returned the gesture and they downed their shots. The whiskey burned but it was a clean taste. Stephen was no expert, but he guessed this hadn't been watered down. Which made it better than what they were selling.

Colin was looking around the room, sizing people up. Stephen felt a flash of annoyance. Of course they waited. What else were they going to do? He was becoming increasingly convinced that Colin was making this up as they went along. He was acting as if everything he said was arcane wisdom from the master rumrunners, but Stephen hadn't seen him do anything he couldn't have figured out himself. He was starting to think that this was as easy as falling off a log.

"Good evening, boys," said a soft contralto behind them. "Frank says you have something for me?"

Stephen turned and could almost feel his breath catch in his throat. She was stunning in a sleek red dress with black accents and a fringe that danced around her thighs as she moved. Her black hair wasn't cut in a short bob to follow fashion. It fell in a lush cascade down one side of her neck, held in place by a pearled band.

He had never seen such a beautiful woman in his life.

She looked back and forth between the brothers as if unsure which of them she was meant to be talking to. Stephen's instincts took over and told him it absolutely must not be Colin.

"We do," he said, stepping forward to offer her his hand. "Colin, could I have the flask please?"

Colin just raised an eyebrow and smiled. "Of course, sir," he said, and Stephen heard the mocking tone in his voice. He hoped she hadn't noticed it.

"Stephen Ridley," he said as they shook hands. "My brother Colin. You must be Melissa."

"Estes," she said. "I manage the club." She noticed Stephen hadn't quite let go of her hand. "What's in the flask?" she prompted.

Stephen gathered his wits and took the flask from Colin's outstretched hand. Colin gave him a look, but Stephen ignored it.

"Your bartender tells me you're out of gin." He opened the flask and offered it to her. "It's not the best quality, but it's gin, and there's more where this came from."

She raised the flask to her lips and took a sip. Stephen studied her as she rolled the gin around her mouth and swallowed it.

"No, it's not the best," she said, "but we've sold worse. How much have you got?"

"How long will a hundred bottles last you?"

She smiled. "Not long enough. Gin and rum are always short. Can you get more?"

"A steady supply of both. Better quality too."

Melissa smiled. "Well that's intriguing. We don't get too many Englishmen here. Where'd you come in from?"

"A little place at the edge of the Bahamas," said Stephen. "You won't have heard of it."

She laughed, and Stephen felt a little rush of pleasure. "No," she said, "you're probably right. But you've got a fast boat somewhere nearby, loaded up with this, and that's all that matters. Why don't you have your brother work out terms with Frank, and we'll talk about your plans."

Stephen offered her his arm, and she took it.

"Talk to Frank, Colin," he said as they stepped away from the bar.

Colin laughed and shook his head. "I'm getting the short end of this deal," he muttered after them. "No offense to Frank."

Melissa took him outside onto the wooden walkway that led down to the docks. The noise of the bar faded somewhat as the doors closed behind them.

"Your first time here?" Melissa asked.

"That's right."

"Where'd you pick up my name?"

"From another runner," said Stephen. "He was headed south of here, but he said we should look you up. I'm glad we did."

"So am I," she said. She stopped, and they leaned against a railing and looked out at the boats riding softly on the moonlit water. "Our last supplier got himself picked off by the Coast Guard, and our stock's running low. There's plenty of places down the coast for someone with a thirst to quench. We've got a good business here, but it won't last if we can't supply the product. Mr. Kusack won't be happy."

"Who's that?"

She looked at him with surprise. "You don't know?"

Stephen shrugged. "Saw the name on some signs on the way here. That's all I know."

"Well, Ellis Kusack owns just about everything in Harmony Beach. That includes this place. I'm just the manager. He's a big deal of a businessman from up north. Tons of money, and he's investing it down here. He owns the club, most of the land, that big estate you saw going up at the south end of the island."

"Didn't see that," said Stephen.

She grinned. "God knows how you missed it. I've seen the drawings. The Vanderbilts will have nothing on this place when it's done."

They looked out over the water. Behind them, the sound of the band filtered out through the glass. Stephen could feel the dock boards gently vibrating through the soles of his shoes.

"I grew up here," Melissa said after a few moments. "Not many around here can say that. It's nice having some money for a change, but I do miss the quiet. I used to come out here this time of night in an old dinghy my father fixed up for me. Bring a boy out sometimes. Sit there and watch the stars, listen to the boat creak. Whatever else happened."

"I had to go five islands over to find a girlfriend," Stephen said. "Her name was Evadne."

"Really? What kind of name is that?"

"It's from a Greek myth. She's married to this great warrior who brags that not even Zeus can stop him from conquering Thebes. So Zeus gets ticked off, as he does, and blows the guy to bits with a lightning bolt. Evadne throws herself on his funeral pyre and dies."

Melissa struggled to hold back her laughter. "That's…that's terrible!"

"Her parents were a bit odd. The whole family had names like that. But the rest were all boys, so Evadne was it. She looked like the Kaiser, and there was something wrong with her ears. Had no sea legs at all. The moment she got in a boat she'd get sick."

"Oh no! What did you do?"

"Well, there was a little uninhabited spot of land a couple miles away that we'd go to. But by the time we got there, she'd been vomiting over the side for the last half hour, and when I kissed her, she tasted terrible."

Melissa laughed. "Well, you obviously need to range a little farther from home."

"Yes," said Stephen, "I can see the selection's much better here."

"Then you'll have to come back. If you can really get your hands on a steady supply of decent rum and gin, I'll take as much as you can bring in."

"We can," said Stephen. "So it's just a question of money then."

She edged closer to him. "Frank can handle that."

WHEN THEY ARRIVED at a price per bottle, Colin did some quick math to work out how much they'd just made for the load and had to hold back a whistle. It was a lot of money.

"So," said Frank. "Where's the stuff?"

"We landed on the channel side," said Colin. "Couple miles down the shore."

Frank chuckled. "Trying to be discreet, huh? All right, I'll round up a couple boys to help load and send the truck down. But next time you can just pull up to the dock. Hell of a lot easier. Mr. Kusack's got an understanding with the Sheriff. He's got an understanding with most everyone around here. You won't have any trouble."

"Next time?" said Colin. "So we're in business?"

"Assume that's what Melissa's working out with your brother. Like she said, our last supplier got himself picked up by the Coast Guard. You came along at a good time. Of course if you want to go looking for other buyers…"

"No," Colin said hurriedly. "I like your price. We'll be back."

"All right," said Frank, "let's go find your boat."

Frank led the way to the club's storage room and rounded up a couple burly looking men, apparently unoccupied, throwing dice against the back wall. A few minutes later, they'd found Stephen as well and loaded everyone into a wooden bodied Ford Depot Hack. Frank drove, and Colin sat up front with him. Stephen and the two sullenly quiet workers sat in the back.

"Tell me where," said Frank as they drove south out of Harmony Beach. Colin studied the trees until he saw a stand that looked familiar.

"Off to the right along here."

Frank pulled off the road, and the truck immediately started to spin its wheels in the sandy soil. He wrestled it onto a rockier patch of ground and cut the engine. "How far to your boat?"

"Those mangroves over there." Colin pointed them out. They were perhaps two hundred yards away.

Frank shook his head. "Seriously, just come to the dock next time."

They trudged through the sand and marsh into the mangroves, and Colin led them down the gentle rise to where *Pegasus* lay moored. From there it was a simple enough operation. They unloaded the burlocks onto the shore in a neat pile and counted them. Frank sliced open a couple and inspected the bottles. Once he opened a bottle and took a quick swallow, then passed the bottle to his two silent stevedores.

When the load was ashore, each of them lifted a burlock with each hand and trudged back up the sand to where they'd left the truck. It took several trips to get them all loaded, and Colin was feeling the exertion by the time the last of the bottles was stacked in the back of the truck.

"Well boys, you're real smugglers now," said Frank, leaning against the truck. "Rumrunners. How's it feel?"

"Nah," Stephen said. "We're not real rumrunners until we get paid!"

"Fair enough," said Frank. He took a thick envelope from his pocket and handed it over to Colin as the stevedores climbed back into the truck.

"There you go. You did good. Keep it up, stay away from the Coast Guard, and keep your noses clean. Bring us good quality product, and you'll make some money. We'll both have a good thing here."

He climbed up into the truck. "And like I said, for hell's sake, just dock at the club next time."

They watched the truck turn around and head back north. As the sound of its engine faded into the distance, Colin opened the envelope and riffled the cash before Stephen's face. Then they were both laughing, hugging each other, jumping up and down in the road like a pair of children.

Finally they calmed down enough to make their way back to *Pegasus*.

"I think you enjoyed that," said Colin as they untied from the trees and poled the boat back out into the channel. "It's not just the money. I think you liked that. I think you want to do it again."

"Yeah, we better come back," said Stephen. "I've got a date."

8

DAWN WAS JUST BEGINNING TO COLOR THE SKY AS *PEGASUS* PULLED up to the dock at Beckers Cay. No one was there to meet them. They tied up the boat and headed up the slope toward the house, a dark shape looming out of the murky pre-dawn.

Colin was tired. It had been a long night, but it had been worth it. He'd been afraid that something would go wrong, that he'd not only get himself in serious trouble, but also Stephen. And worse, that he'd blow their best chance to get out of debt and provide for their mother. But the run had gone off without a hitch. With every step, he felt the thick bundle of money pulling against his heavy cotton shirt.

The house was dark as they approached. "Let's keep quiet," Stephen said softly. "Don't want to wake mother. I could use some sleep myself."

"No kidding," Colin replied.

They made their way quietly up the stairs. Stephen disappeared into his room and closed the door. Colin found the door to his old room farther down the hall. There was just enough light from the window to save him from bumping into the furniture. He found an old lamp on the table by the door but had to refill it from a nearly empty bottle of oil.

The place was dusty, unkempt. It looked mostly like he'd left it, though mother had apparently stored a few things here, piling them haphazardly on his bed. Colin cleaned them off and lay down on top of the covers. There was no point in looking for other clothes. Anything still in the drawers of the dresser against the far wall wouldn't be his.

It was odd to be back here, he thought as he faded toward sleep, especially after the things he'd said when he left. But there was the money, still there in his shirt pocket. Like mother had said, ready money solved most problems.

And then Colin was asleep.

It was midday by the time he awoke. He found Emily downstairs, shooing Marcus's wife out the door.

"I'm fine," she said, "just fine. You're a dear but go take care of your own. I'm fine, I tell you."

Then she turned from the door and looked at him with a subtle smile. "It's good to see you here, son," she said. Colin knew she was expressing much more than relief that they'd made it safely back.

Colin nodded and hugged her.

"It's good to be back," he murmured in her ear. And he realized it wasn't just what she wanted to hear. It was true.

"Well look at you two." Stephen came down the stairs smiling. "Haven't seen you this happy in a while," he said to Emily.

"Everything went okay?" she asked.

Stephen smiled. "We nailed it. Put us together, we can do just about anything."

Colin clapped him on the shoulder. "New future," he said. "Starting now. Let's make things different."

THEIR FIRST MOVE was back to Nassau to pay off Joe. They arrived around midday and found her in her shed. Colin enjoyed her look of surprise as they walked in and handed her the sheaf of bills.

"Already? Thought it would take you longer than that."

"Maybe you should go into business with us," Colin joked. "You got a fast boat?"

Joe laughed. "I've got money enough for now," she said. "But if I manage to blow it all on some damn fool scheme, I'll look you up."

On the way back, Colin steered off course and headed deeper into the islands. Stephen had been lounging in the forward cockpit, but now he made his way back and dropped in beside Colin.

"Where are we going?"

"Big Spring, of course," said Colin. "I assume that's where you meant to get this supply of high quality booze you promised Melissa?"

Stephen grinned and nodded. "Beats buying it off the Rum Line. Simon doesn't water down his stuff. He'll have all we need, cheaper, and better too. We can make the run direct from his place and skip the line completely."

Colin laughed. He'd thought it through and already knew that Stephen was right. Simon Bonamy had been distilling rum from homegrown sugar and molasses on Big Spring Cay since before they were born. He'd originally sold to locals around the islands. As more British travelers arrived in the Bahamas, he'd grown his own juniper crop as well and branched out to produce gin. Colin had no doubt that Simon could produce enough volume to fill *Pegasus* every few days. It would be higher quality than what they'd gotten from the sailors on the Rum Line, even before they'd watered theirs down. It wouldn't have any of the appropriate tax stamps, but prohibition had rendered that issue moot. It was a good plan.

Of course, there was the matter of Simon's personal eccentricities.

"You got your passport with you?" Colin asked.

"You didn't say we were going today," Stephen protested.

Colin laughed and patted his shirt pocket. "Don't worry. I brought them."

"Good," Stephen laughed. "We can't run to Harmony Beach if he sinks our boat!"

Simon lived in the remains of a long-abandoned Royal Navy resupply station, though he insisted it was a fortress. The crumbling stone structure had an old black powder cannon on the outer wall overlooking the sea, and somehow Simon had kept it in operating order. He'd been known to fire it at boats when annoyed, though thankfully he'd never actually hit anything.

All this supported Simon's claim that Big Spring Cay was an independent country, with himself as head of state. Colin suspected that was mainly to justify his refusal to pay excise duties on his alcohol. Incredibly, it seemed to work. The authorities had tried to collect from him from time to time, but they generally found it not worth the trouble.

As part of Simon's claim to independence, he issued Big Spring Cay passports. Simon put applicants through an exhaustive, and frequently changing, process to get one of his passports. Landing on Big Spring without one was not recommended. Getting one, on the other hand, had become something of a rite of passage among the local islanders. It meant you were old enough to drink on your own.

Within the hour, they'd reached Big Spring Cay. It was a small, flat bit of land, a low line of trees above the water with Simon's fortress at one end. Colin reduced speed and came in slowly. As they approached the dock, they saw Simon walking down the dock to meet them. He was of uncertain age, but Colin knew he had to be in his sixties at least. His hair was gray and sparse, and he was bone thin. He carried an old Lee-Enfield rifle in one hand.

Stephen tossed Simon the mooring rope, but he ignored it and let it fall to his feet.

"This is the independent Principality of Big Spring Cay!" Simon shouted. "Who goes there?"

"Oh, come on, Simon," Colin called back. "You know who we are."

Simon shouldered the rifle, and Stephen stepped back. "Whoa, watch out!"

"Border's closed to foreigners," Simon snapped. "Too many spies."

"We're not foreigners!" Colin shouted. "It's Colin and Stephen Ridley. Let me show you our passports!"

"Come on up and show me then," said Simon, but he didn't lower the rifle.

The passports were creased and heavily folded sheets of paper with their names and a few official sounding phrases in Simon's scrawled handwriting. Colin carefully unfolded them and showed them to him.

Simon carefully examined them. "All right, then," he finally said and lowered the rifle. "Welcome home citizens. How's your mother doing?"

"She's fine, thank you," Colin answered. "What the hell was that about, Simon? You've known us since we were kids."

Simon grinned, showing his few remaining teeth. "Sorry about that. Got to do things by the book these days. These are troubled times."

"Yeah," said Stephen as they walked back up the dock. "What's this about spies?"

"Couple foreigners showed up a while back," said Simon. "Said they were here to buy all the rum I can make. Going to take it to America. Didn't want to meet my price though. Started throwing their weight around. One of them pulled a gun on me. In my own country! Had to call out the militia. Sent them packing right enough. Put an eight-pound ball into their hull too. They won't be back."

"Jesus, Simon! You actually shot a boat with that thing?" Colin couldn't believe it. "You'll have the Navy down on you! They can't ignore that!"

Simon just laughed. "Those boys? I don't think they'll be talking to the foreign authorities. Get themselves arrested before me."

"Hope you're right," said Stephen.

"So what brings you?" Simon asked. They were approaching the fort. One of Simon's crew drove past in a cart full of fresh sugar cane from the fields. The smell of the fires and the cane presses was strong.

"Well, don't get excited," said Colin, "but we're here to buy as much rum as you can make so we can take it to America. But we'll pay a fair price," he quickly added.

Simon laughed. "You boys are running rum? Didn't think that was legal."

"It's not exactly," Colin admitted.

"And you were such good boys," Simon said, shaking his head. "Hate to have to put you in jail." Then he grinned. "No law against it here. Come inside and let's talk."

By SUNSET, they had a deal with Simon and a full load of rum and gin aboard *Pegasus*. Simon had given them a bargain price on this load as thanks for introducing him to burlocks. They were a huge improvement over the wooden crates he'd been using, as well as less expensive, and Simon was delighted.

They shared a dinner of conch stew and pigeon peas, and then Simon walked them down to the dock. He bade them goodbye and stamped their Big Spring passports with a hand carved wooden stamp. Colin fired up the engine, and *Pegasus* headed out toward Florida.

The crossing was uneventful. They steered well clear of the clutch of freighters on the Rum Line. They saw no Coast Guard cutters or other rumrunners. They saw nothing but the sea and the moon until the lights of Harmony Beach appeared.

Colin came in slow toward the docks at the Motorboat Club. A dockhand stood at the end of a pier and waved them in with a flashlight. He caught the rope Stephen tossed him and helped them moor.

"Welcome to the Harmony Beach Motorboat Club," he said as they climbed up. "How can we help you tonight?" His eye swept across the stack of burlocks. He clearly already knew the answer.

"Here to see Frank," said Colin.

The man nodded. "I'll let him know you're here." He left them with the boat and hurried up the dock toward the club.

"Huh. This *is* a lot easier," said Stephen.

A minute later, the dockhand returned with Frank and Melissa. Colin saw Stephen beam as she appeared.

"You made it!" she said. "It's good to see you again. Any trouble?"

Colin shook his head. "Quiet out there tonight."

"Glad to hear it. So what have you brought me?"

Stephen took a burlock from the cockpit and sliced it open with his knife. "You're going to like this," he said. He opened a bottle of Simon's best rum and handed it to her. She sniffed it, then took a swig and passed the bottle to Frank. They did the same with a bottle of gin. Frank nodded his approval.

"Frank, can you get a couple guys down and move this stuff up to the back room? Colin, you can handle this part yourself, can't you? Something I need to discuss with your brother."

And then she was leading Stephen up the dock toward the club. Frank traded a look with Colin, then headed up himself, leaving Colin alone.

"Figures," he muttered to himself, "he goes off to have fun and leaves me to do the work." Then he smiled to himself. "Guess it's his turn."

Soon, Frank returned with two men and a cart. Colin handed burlocks up to Frank. Frank passed them to one of his longshoremen, and the other one stacked them on the cart.

"So where's this Kusack fellow?" Colin asked as they worked. "If he owns the place, I'd expect him to take more of an interest in it."

"Mr. Kusack's up north," said Frank, "managing his business interests. He's up there a lot. But he'll be back soon. Never away too long. And he does take an interest. He'll want to meet new runners. Especially you two."

Colin hauled two more burlocks out and hefted them up to the dock. He wondered what made them different from other runners. But something about the way Frank had said that told him not to push the point right now.

MELISSA GIGGLED and fell back against Stephen's bare chest. "Stop that," she said, slapping his roaming hand in mock annoyance. "We've got plenty of time."

Stephen allowed himself to be dissuaded. He let his arms fall to his sides, soaking in the luxury of her silk sheets, the brush of her hair against his skin, the curve of her bare back.

"So," she said, "how did that compare to poor Evadne?"

"Who?"

She grinned and kissed him. "Good answer."

They were upstairs at the back of the club, in what he assumed were Melissa's private quarters. The bed was a huge four-poster shrouded in gauzy curtains. They looked out at open doors onto a small balcony and the sea beyond.

"So you live here at the club?" Stephen asked.

"I've got my own place in the village," she said. "But I stay here most nights. It's nicer. Ellis spares no expense. He doesn't have to."

"Ellis? You mean Kusack? Guess he's a pretty big deal."

She snuggled against him. "He changed everything around here, all right. I used to run a little fisherman's bar here if you can believe it. Not much more than a shack. It blew down every time a big storm came through, and we'd have to rebuild it. Just barely eked out a living. Then prohibition came along, and there wasn't even that anymore."

Melissa fell silent for a moment. Stephen felt the slow and steady rhythm of her breathing. "Then Ellis showed up, and it started raining money. He bought the bar, knocked it down and...all this. He hired pretty much everybody in Harmony Beach. Started staking out lots and selling them to folks from up north with more money than sense. Building on them for the new owners. Talked the state into paying him to build the new bridge and improve the road. And of course he's building his palace down at south end. Times are changing."

"For the better?"

She thought about it for a moment. "More money, that's for sure. A lot more exciting than it used to be. But I used to really run my place. Supposedly I own this place, but really I work for him. I pay him back for the construction, plus protection money and guaranteed supply. He gets all the profits."

She rolled over to look into his face. "He'll want to see you and your brother when he gets back," she said. Stephen could see the sudden intensity in her eyes. "Be careful with him. He's got his fingers in everything here. When he sees something, he wants it." She paused. "And when he wants something, he gets it. He'll want you in his pocket too."

"Not going to happen," said Stephen. "My brother and I work for ourselves. If that's not good enough for him..."

She smiled and kissed him. "I hope you're right."

9

After the second run, the rumrunning business fell into a steady pattern for a while as they learned more about how to build a steady and reliable operation.

They began by paying back wages to the farm workers along with a bonus for their badly stretched patience. That went a long way toward settling any concerns on Beckers Cay about the family's new life of crime. Not that the objections had been serious to begin with. America was a long way away, and nobody was quite sure why they'd want to forbid a man from having a good drink or two at the end of a long day's work.

Colin and Stephen soon realized things would be easier and more efficient if they staged their cargo at Beckers Cay and ran to Florida directly from there. The farmhands were put to work restoring crumbling storage sheds and building a raised loading ramp to help bring heavy loads up from the dock. Marcus and a few others began making periodic runs to Big Spring Cay in one of the fishing boats, bringing back more than *Pegasus* could carry in a single load.

The renewed industry quickly spread across the island. The residents began repairing decaying homes. Women sang songs to their babies to the rhythm of hammers and saws. Boats showed up with supplies from Nassau. Stephen sensed an atmosphere of hope that he hadn't felt on the island in a long time.

In particular, he noticed that his mother was smiling more than she had since his father had died. If nothing else, she loved having Colin back, and she enjoyed seeing her two sons getting along and working together. He saw her straightening up things around the house, dusting off old antiques, and making a list of furniture to replace the things they'd sold off. She saw a path back to the life they'd once had, and Stephen was proud that he'd helped give her that.

And of course he had his own reasons to smile.

On each run, Colin would get the cargo unloaded and collect the money while Stephen and Melissa retreated to her suite above the office. There had been other girls before; the unfortunate Evadne was a bit of an exaggeration. But Melissa was like no woman he'd ever known before. At home he would suddenly stop and remember something she'd said, or nights in her bed with the breeze off the sea cooling their skin. He wasn't entirely sure, but he suspected this might be what it was to fall in love.

That sounded silly. He hardly knew her. They met every few days for a romp in a bar. He tried to tell himself it was the excitement of smuggling that created that electricity between them. But he wasn't convinced.

Three weeks later, the sheds were repaired and full of Simon's best. Stephen had just returned from a supply run to Nassau with something extra in his pocket. It was a silver bracelet he'd spotted and bought for Melissa. He touched the small box with a combination of excitement and dread. What if this was just a bit of fun for her? What if he made his sincerity clear and she thought it was ridiculous? What if she laughed at him?

He kept the bracelet to himself as they loaded *Pegasus* and launched into the setting sun. Colin *would* laugh at him. Stephen was unusually quiet as they crossed the dark sea toward Harmony Beach.

~

COLIN CUT the throttle back and came slowly into the dock at the Motorboat Club. It had been a good run. The weather was mild, and the seas were calm. The Coast Guard was still out there looking for rumrunners, but they'd seen no sign of the *Mojave* tonight.

Two dockhands waited for them. As Colin brought the boat in toward the slip, he saw one run back up toward the club. By the time they moored, Frank had returned with a couple of his stevedores. There was a tension about him that Colin hadn't seen before.

"Evening," Colin said as he climbed up onto the dock. "How's business, Frank?"

"We'll get this unloaded," said Frank. "Mr. Kusack wants to meet you." He paused for a moment, then added, "*Both* of you."

So the mysterious Ellis Kusack was back in town. The man in charge. Well, there was no reason for that to change things, Colin told himself. He needed liquor, and they could provide a good product at a good price.

Then Frank leaned in and murmured, "Keep a tight hand on your brother."

That stopped Colin cold. He thought he detected a bit of fear in Frank's eyes. What the hell was going on?

He just nodded and said, "Okay. Let's go meet Mr. Kusack." He turned to Stephen and murmured, "Best behavior. And keep your eyes open. Something's up."

They walked up the dock, and Frank led them inside. At first things seemed normal. The music was loud and raucous. Couples one-stepped on the floor or did the Charleston. Drinkers lined the bar two deep.

But then Colin noticed the large table in a back corner. The other tables had been pulled away to give it its own space. Frank led them toward it, and Colin saw men in suits at the edges of that space, watching. Others lounged in armchairs with women in beaded dresses hanging off them.

One man was at the center of it all, holding court with the others arrayed around him. That had to be Ellis Kusack. He was a large, stocky man with a boxer's face and a cigar in one hand. He made quick, stabbing gestures with it as he told some story that he obviously thought was extremely funny.

And the woman on his arm, looking at them nervously as they approached…that was Melissa.

Colin felt Stephen tense at his side, and he put a hand on his brother's forearm. Melissa gave them a tense look and a subtle motion of her head.

A moment later, Kusack himself noticed them. He stood up, throwing his arms wide, and beamed at them. "This is the guys! There they are!"

Another man stood up at Kusack's right. He was younger than Kusack, lean and muscular, and he wasn't smiling. His eyes swept efficiently across both of them. Colin had seen eyes like those during the war, looking out of the gaunt faces of men who'd seen and done too much killing. *That one's a soldier*, he told himself. Colin also spotted the gun under his jacket.

"Come here, come here!" Kusack was saying. "Boys, a couple chairs for my new rumrunners! Frank, get them something to drink!"

Frank nodded. "Right away, Mr. Kusack." He hurried off toward the bar.

Two other men vacated their chairs, but as Colin and Stephen approached, the soldier stepped around Kusack and stopped them. Colin was the closer.

"Arms out," the soldier said and demonstrated the pose he wanted. "Like this."

Colin complied, and the soldier frisked him, quickly but expertly. Then he moved on to Stephen and repeated the process. For a moment, Colin worried he'd find the pistol Stephen had pulled on Scogins back on the Rum Line. But apparently Stephen wasn't carrying it tonight. He did take a small box from Stephen's pocket, and Colin saw his brother tense. But the soldier decided it wasn't a threat and put it back where he'd found it.

"Joe, Joe, what the hell are you doing?" Kusack said suddenly. "These are friends! We're all partners here. Back off already."

He turned to shake Colin's hand, and then Stephen's. "Ellis Kusack," he said, "damn glad to make your acquaintance. This is Joe Stoski, my head of security. Don't mind him. He takes his job a little too seriously sometimes. Sit down, sit down!"

Stoski moved silently back to his seat. Colin noticed Kusack hadn't stopped him until after his search was finished.

They sat down, and Frank returned with cocktails. Colin could sense the nervous energy pouring off Stephen as he glared at Melissa. Melissa ignored him, busily hanging on whatever Kusack said or did. Colin quickly scanned the others at the table. Two looked like Stoski's men, young toughs who were armed and silently watched. The others Colin pegged as friends of Kusack. They were older, less fit, dressed like tourists on a Florida vacation.

"We're all glad you two showed up when you did," Kusack was saying. "Aren't we, doll?"

"We sure are, Ellis," said Melissa.

"The last guy we had went and got himself picked off by the Coast Guard. We were damn near dry when you came along. That wouldn't do, would it fellows?"

There was a round of laughter from the guests. The bodyguards laughed politely and again said nothing.

"Sure wish I'd been here when you showed up, though," Kusack said. "Melissa here runs the place for me. Does a hell of a job. But she doesn't know the business outside the club. The connections, the costs. We got to work out some new details."

Colin didn't like the sound of that. "What details are those?"

Kusack drained his cocktail and handed the glass to Melissa. "Get me another one of these, will you, baby?"

"Sure, Ellis." Melissa took the empty glass back toward the bar. Stephen watched her go.

"Well, I'm sure you noticed landing's a lot easier here than what you might be used to," said Kusack when she was gone. "That's because we've got an understanding with the local Sheriff. But that doesn't come without strings. Nothing does, right? This place is growing fast. He's had to take on more deputies."

"I see," said Colin.

"You're safe here, but that costs. Lot of other costs that don't show up on the club books. Bad news is that means we can't keep the price she offered."

Colin said nothing, tried not to react at all. Here it came. The squeeze.

"There's another problem," Kusack added.

"We're listening."

"I've got to be able to control the quality of the product," said Kusack. "People expect the best here. If we don't give it to them, they'll go somewhere else. Now when we were desperate for booze, Melissa did what she had to do to keep the bar open. But I won't risk my reputation on product I don't know."

Colin turned and traded a look with Stephen.

"I got a supplier I trust. He brings product out to the Rum Line. I know his stuff. It's good booze. I want you to buy from him from now on."

Stephen erupted. "What the hell are you talking about? Our product's top shelf! We've seen the watered down shit they sell on the line. Ours is ten times better."

"That's what you say," said Kusack, and his expression was a lot less friendly now. "But I don't know you. Couple of foreigners showing up with stuff that could come from anywhere. I got to control the quality of the booze I sell in my club."

Colin saw it all now. They were taking good money out of Harmony Beach, and Kusack didn't like that. As far as he was concerned, everything in Harmony Beach belonged to him—including Melissa from the looks of it. He was intent on squeezing all their profits out and taking them for himself. This supplier on the Rum Line was doubtless one of Kusack's own operations. The prices would be inflated with the skim going straight back to Kusack, even as he squeezed them for protection on this end. When he was done with them, they'd be little more than employees. And poorly paid ones at that.

"Mr. Kusack," Colin said calmly, "we've played fair with your people in your absence. You've got a good thing going with us if you stop and take a good look. We'd hate to walk away from that and go somewhere else with our liquor." He let that hang there for a few seconds. "But my brother and I have a business to run just like you. And we'll decide what we're going to buy and sell."

He could see that Kusack wasn't used to not getting what he wanted. He looked them over for a long moment, Stephen in particular. Stephen wasn't saying anything, but his expression, his posture, everything about him signaled anger and defiance. Stoski had picked up on it too. He was still seated, but there was a tension in his body. He was poised to spring if Stephen made a move. Colin leaned over and put a hand on Stephen's forearm.

"Isn't that right, Stephen?"

"Yeah," Stephen said, his voice terse and clipped. "That's right."

Kusack sat back and clipped the end off a new cigar. "Well," he said, "that's too bad. Really too bad. I was hoping we could work together."

"I wouldn't worry," said Colin. "I'm sure you'll find someone out there to take your deal. As for us, there's plenty of thirsty people out there, and plenty of places to land. No reason for us to get in each other's way, is there?"

Kusack considered it for a moment. "No reason at all," he said at last. "But I'd be careful out there if I was you. The guy you replaced didn't end up so well."

Colin saw Melissa returning with Kusack's drink. Kusack spotted it as well, and Colin sensed the wheels turning behind his dark eyes.

"They ought to have your boat unloaded by now," said Kusack. "Frank'll have your money. No reason to keep you any longer."

Colin set his glass down on the table and stood up. "Thanks for the drink," he said.

Stephen said nothing, but he tensed as Melissa returned to the table, and Colin steered him away. They headed for the doors.

Frank was on the dock as they returned to the *Pegasus*. He handed Colin a sheaf of bills. "Sorry," he said quietly, mainly to Stephen. "Probably should have told you how it lies."

"Yeah," said Stephen, "that would have been good to know."

"Water under the bridge," said Colin before Stephen could say something else. "Take care of yourself, Frank."

"You too."

Then they climbed aboard the boat. Frank cast off the mooring line, and Colin steered away from the dock. Stephen said nothing. He just sat looking straight ahead over the bow, out to the dark sea.

As the lights of Harmony Beach receded behind them, Stephen took the small box that Stoski had discovered out of his pocket. He looked at it for a long moment, then flipped it over the side.

"What was that?" Colin asked.

"Nothing."

THE TRIP BACK WAS QUIET. STEPHEN FUMED. COLIN CONSIDERED what to do next. There weren't many good answers. The Harmony Beach opportunity had fallen into their laps. It had given them all the money they needed and absorbed all the cargo they could handle. They hadn't lined up other buyers. Now they had liquor flowing in from Simon, and nowhere to sell it.

They needed a new customer.

The next day, they toured the sheds and took stock of their inventory.

"We can tell Simon to slow down," said Colin.

"He won't like it," said Stephen. "We promised him so much a month."

Colin knew his brother was right. Simon would forgive them, but it would cost them his trust. The next time they came to him for liquor, he'd be harder to deal with. He shrugged. "Or we can just let it pile up here and trust we'll find a buyer."

"How long before we run out of money?" Stephen asked. "Just buying and holding it?"

Colin did some quick calculations. "Not right away," he

decided at last. "A month. Six weeks. We'll have something worked out by then. I'm more worried about you."

Stephen looked up in surprise. "What do you mean?"

"You were pretty upset last night."

"Yeah, funny that."

"It happens," said Colin. "I'm sorry you got burned, but it happens. Just forget about her and move on. There's better women out there."

Stephen bristled at that. "How are we going to find a new buyer?" he asked, turning away and counting down a row of burlocks.

Colin let him change the subject. If Stephen didn't want to talk about his love life, that was fine with him. More than fine. Things had been going well between them since they started this business. Maybe it was best to just let that particular sleeping dog lie.

"Same way we got the first one," Colin said. "We go out to the Rum Line and see who's buying."

Stephen was halfway down the row of stacked burlocks now, counting off with chopping gestures of one hand.

"That's not exactly how we did it," he called back. "We weren't selling there. We were buying."

"So we look for someone like us."

The next night, they loaded up *Pegasus* and headed out to the Rum Line. It looked like it had the last time they were here. Only the ships had changed. There was no sign of the *General Matorras*, which Colin figured was just as well. He doubted they'd be welcome there after the incident with Scogins.

They cruised slowly down the line, sizing up the freighters.

"Looks like the party's over there," Stephen said, pointing out an American flagged tramp steamer, the *Laura Belle*. She was strung with lights and they could hear the music over the water. She was surrounded by a flotilla of small craft, including a half dozen small boats serving as taxis.

"You know what else is different?" Colin said as they approached. "Last time, we showed up empty."

Stephen glanced over his shoulder at the stacked burlocks of rum and gin. They both knew how much those were worth. If they just left them floating around out here, they might be a powerful temptation.

"Someone needs to keep an eye on the boat," Stephen concluded.

"What I was thinking."

Colin cut the engine and let the boat drift into the scattered collection of smaller boats. "Flip you for it?" said Colin, digging a coin out of his pocket.

But Stephen shook his head. "No, you go. You're the better salesman."

He reached behind his back and pulled out his Colt Hammerless. "Besides, I've got this if someone wants the cargo."

"Don't think it'll come to that," said Colin. But then he grinned and pulled out a Webley Bull Dog pistol. "But I took a lesson from last time."

Colin put the gun back in his pocket. "Let's not use these, all right?"

A water taxi pulled up alongside. "Headed for the *Laura Belle?*" the boatman shouted.

"Good luck," Stephen said. "I'll be out here."

Colin smiled. "I'll bring you back a drink."

Stephen laughed and nodded toward the boat full of liquor. "I got a drink! Bring back some money."

THE TAXI TOOK Colin to a steep, cantilevered stairway leading up the hull of the *Laura Belle* to the rail. The party was set up outside on the main deck, and sailors brought crates up from below. It looked as though the hold was full. The ship must not have been here very long. Colin bought a drink at the improvised bar forward of the aft deckhouse and flirted with one of the women. There were a half dozen or so of them, pouncing on any new arrivals who looked like they had money.

The one who zeroed in on Colin was named Clara—"Like Clara Bow!" she said with a coquettish purse of her lips. She told him she was from Boston and had come to Florida because she'd heard the place was booming, and she wanted a piece of it. The *Laura Belle*, she told him, had just arrived yesterday with a load of Canadian whiskey, and the Captain had been happy to have her come along. Pretty women were good for business.

Clara turned out to have a great deal of useful information about the going rates for liquor, as well as who was buying and selling. By the time Clara decided she wasn't getting anywhere with him and moved on, Colin figured he'd learned all he needed to know.

It was too bad, really, he thought. She was a charmer, and he could have stood for some companionship. But now wasn't the time. Now was the time for business. And it was hardly fair to leave Stephen guarding the boat while he dallied with her. Of course when the shoe was on the other foot, his brother had been perfectly happy to play while he worked.

Clara had pointed out someone who'd told her he was looking for rum. Colin was making his way across the crowded deck toward his potential purchaser when a familiar voice said, "Well, if it's not my limey buddy! Where's your brother tonight?"

Colin turned, and there was Sam Blake. "Hello Blake," he said as they shook hands. "Stephen's manning the boat. What about you? You're not still stuck out here?"

Blake laughed. "No, no, that's all sorted out. Back to do some business tonight."

"Buying, are you?"

Blake shook his head. "Other side of the bar. Got a deal

mostly landed. Once he decides the stuff's okay, he'll pay up, and I'll be on my way again. You?"

"Same, except we just got here. Any suggestions on who I should talk to? That tip you gave us about Harmony Beach worked out pretty well. For a while anyway."

"Well, you didn't get caught at least," said Blake. "Coast Guard's getting better at this. Net's getting tighter. Harder to slip through. Might be a good idea to stay on this side of the line. Let someone else take the risk."

Then Blake spotted someone across the deck and said, "All right, gotta run. Good luck to you, Ridley."

"Take care, Blake." And then Colin watched him weave through the crowd on the deck.

It took Colin a few minutes to find the potential buyer he'd been aiming for when Blake interrupted him. Then it took a few more minutes to pry him away from the woman he'd latched onto in the meantime.

The buyer called himself Waxman. Based on Clara's tip, Colin had assumed he wanted his cargo delivered to the Florida coast. But Waxman was a runner himself. He had a diesel-powered trawler and a waiting customer somewhere outside Miami. That wasn't what they'd come here to do, but money was money. And, as Blake had reminded him, it was those last twelve miles that brought all the risk. Right now, he and Stephen weren't breaking any laws at all, apart from the missing tax stamps on Simon's rum.

It was true that their load wouldn't bring as much here, but as Colin negotiated with Waxman, he quickly realized they could still turn a very healthy profit over what they were paying Simon. Becoming wholesalers didn't sound like such a bad idea.

A water taxi took them out to Waxman's boat, and then Waxman pulled his boat alongside *Pegasus*. He was eager to get underway. There was a quick sampling, inspection of a couple random burlocks, money changed hands, and then they were helping transfer their cargo to Waxman's boat.

Half an hour later, *Pegasus* was headed home.

"Doesn't get much easier than that," said Colin as they headed east into Bahamian waters. "Hell, we weren't even breaking the law!"

"Guess not," said Stephen. He was lost in his own thoughts. Colin assumed he was still upset about Melissa. Enough money would eventually distract him.

"We don't even need *Pegasus* for this," Colin went on after a moment. "We can use one of the fishers. Marcus's boat, I'm thinking. She'll carry twice as much."

"You want to cut Marcus in?"

"Plenty to go around. And he's already handling the run from Simon's."

"Okay," said Stephen. "He deserves it."

And so the business model changed once again. Colin continued to be surprised by how quickly circumstances shifted. But they'd been able to adapt, and he was confident they could continue to do so.

A few days went by as they overhauled Marcus's boat, *Lenore,* to prepare for the possibility of heavier seas. So far it had been a calm summer, but storm season was coming. Sooner or later their luck would run out. They'd been raised from childhood to keep a close eye on the skies, to read the signs, to know when a big storm was coming. They knew better than to go out to sea in one. But they still prepared in case they got caught out somewhere.

They held a rechristening party for the *Lenore* when they were done. The locals all showed up. Bishop Deveaux, the leader of the local congregation, blessed the boat, and Emily smashed a bottle of Simon's gin on the bow. There was music, singing and dancing, and food. Emily was delighted. Even Stephen seemed to have forgotten about Melissa, at least for the time being.

The next day, Colin, Stephen, and Marcus loaded the boat in the morning and set out around midday for the Rum Line. *Lenore* was no match for *Pegasus'* speed, and they wanted to reach the Rum Line before sunset, when the buyers would show up.

Again, the weather cooperated. Marcus steered the boat, and there was little for Colin and Stephen to do but lounge on top of the small deckhouse and soak up the sun. As they'd planned, they reached the cluster of ships as the sun was just starting to stain the water red. They eased into place near the *Laura Belle* once again. Marcus saw the women beckoning from the railings, and saw a drunken fistfight break out on a nearby boat. He wanted no part of the decadence aboard the ships. So he remained behind with the cargo while Colin and Stephen boarded the *Laura Belle*.

The process of selling cargo proved a simple one. There was an upfront fee paid to the ship for coming aboard and competing with their cargo. But once that was settled, there were plenty of buyers looking for something in addition to the *Laura Belle's* Canadian whiskey. The first buyer didn't take all of their load, but a second took the rest. By midnight, the money had been collected, the cargo transferred, and the boats were on their way, running the gauntlet back to Florida. They turned the *Lenore* in the opposite direction and headed home, arriving not long before sunrise.

That became their pattern for the next few weeks. Two crews of former farmhands made the runs back and forth to Big Spring Cay, bringing in loads and storing them in the farm's sheds. From there, it was loaded aboard *Lenore* and, every two to three days Colin, Stephen, and Marcus would take it out to the Rum Line. When the *Laura Belle* sold out of Canadian whiskey and headed north again, they found another freighter willing to let them sell. They began to recognize familiar faces, to be known around the Rum Line. And the money kept flowing in.

~

STEPHEN WENT FORWARD and dropped the sea anchor while Colin readied the dinghy. They'd realized after the first few trips that there was room aboard the *Lenore* for their own small boat. It was all they needed, and it was more reliable than the water taxis.

Marcus was climbing up onto the roof of the deckhouse as Stephen went aft. He gave Stephen a nod and then sat down in the wooden chair he'd put up there. He'd remain there until they returned, watching over the boat. Nobody had ever molested the *Lenore* here, but Marcus remained deeply suspicious of other runners.

Stephen helped Colin launch the dinghy, and they rowed over to the nearest freighter. He didn't even pay attention to the ships anymore. The names and the flags changed, as did the language of the crew. But the business remained the same.

But something was different this time, Stephen realized as he scanned the makeshift bar in the hold. At a back corner table, two men talked quietly over shot glasses. He saw a sheaf of bills change hands and disappear into a coat pocket. The man doing the paying was Joe Stoski.

Colin didn't seem to have noticed Stoski. He said, "See what you can find and meet me at the bar," and then he was gone.

Stephen turned and walked through the crowd in a straight line toward Stoski's table. Kusack wasn't there. That was odd, Stephen thought. Where would Kusack go without Stoski?

Some instinct made Stoski look up. He tensed as he recognized Stephen.

"Hello, Joe," said Stephen. "How's things?"

Stoski said nothing. The seller was looking at him now, unable to miss the sudden tension. His hand crept toward his pocket.

"Where's the boss tonight?" Stephen asked.

"Up north," Stoski said at last. "Business."

"And he left you here? That doesn't sound right."

"He needed me to take care of some things. He's got a lot of business. More than you, I think."

Stephen smiled, showed his teeth. "Oh we're doing fine. Plenty of business around for everyone."

"Well you won't find any here," said Stoski. He relaxed a bit and picked up his drink. "Why don't you go look somewhere else?" Then he knocked back the shot and set the glass down on the table with a hard click.

"Sure, Joe, sure. Just thought I'd say hi for old times' sake."

"Not necessary."

Stephen turned his back and walked away. He was shaking, he realized, not with fear, but with anger. It was welling up inside him, and he didn't know what to do with it. He went to the bar, ordered a shot of whiskey, and downed it. He thought to wait for Colin, but five minutes later, there was still no sign of his brother. And an idea had been forming in the back of Stephen's mind. Finally he swore and pushed off from the bar. It wasn't as though Colin consulted him on deals. He could damn well make his own.

Stephen had learned to tell the runners from those buyers who just ran a speakeasy somewhere and needed their product delivered. They dressed differently, carried themselves differently. By now Stephen could pick them out from across the crowded hold. He spotted someone who didn't have the harder edge about him that Stephen associated with runners. He walked up to him with his hand out.

"You look like someone who needs a few good stiff drinks delivered ashore."

He was right. The guy ran a place up by Jupiter Inlet, and he was nervous as hell. Stephen had to tell him they were outside the territorial limit, and nobody was going to arrest him here. Gradually he drew out what the guy needed and what he could pay for it. It was a simple run. *Pegasus* could handle the load easily. The buyer just didn't have a fast enough boat. He'd come out here in a sailing skiff.

"We can take care of you," Stephen said. "Half now, half on delivery. Tomorrow night okay?"

The customer nodded, eager to be done with this. "Yeah, tomorrow night's fine."

"We'll be there."

"You did what?"

Colin put his drink down on the bar and took a deep breath. The drunk to his left turned and muttered something about keeping it down.

Stephen shrugged. "We're here to make money, right? I got us a run."

Colin leaned in and lowered his voice. "We're not here to do runs! We've got a load to sell here."

"Did you sell it?"

Colin sighed. "Yeah, I found a buyer. He liked the samples. We have to take him out to look it over and then we get paid."

"All right, then. That's your deal. Tomorrow we load up *Pegasus* and close my deal. Marcus can have a night off."

Colin was worried. On the surface it made sense. They'd meant to run liquor to the coast from the beginning, and this sounded like a straightforward run for a customer who might become a steady source of revenue. But Colin knew his brother. He could practically see the nervous energy pouring out of him. Something else was going on.

"What aren't you telling me, Stephen?"

Stephen said nothing for a long moment. Then he finally let out a breath. "Yeah, okay," he said. "Joe Stoski's here."

"Yeah, I know," said Colin. "I steered clear of him."

"I didn't. Turns out Kusack's out of town. Up north dealing with his businesses."

"So?"

"So you're making the delivery tomorrow night. After you drop me at Harmony Beach."

Colin couldn't believe it. "Ah, son of a..." He picked up his drink, but the glass was empty, so he slammed it back down on the bar and waved for the bartender. "God damn it, Stephen! Don't get involved with that girl. She's a dead end."

"She's going to explain some things to me," Stephen practically hissed. "And then I've got some things to say to her. I'm going."

"So you committed us to a run. You committed *me* to make it while you're off having a fight with...where do you get off? Why am I going to do this?"

"We already took his deposit, Colin. We do what we say we're going to do."

Colin shook his head. He'd put some effort into building up a reputation for reliability, and he didn't want to risk that. And it wasn't as if he couldn't handle the run himself. But damn it. Stephen was losing his head over this woman—this gangster's woman he reminded himself. Colin didn't see any good ending there. The best thing to do would be to talk Stephen out of it, but he'd seen that look in his brother's eye before. He knew he wasn't going to talk Stephen out of it.

As THE SUN began to set the next day, they loaded *Pegasus* and tied down the burlocks. They worked quietly, speaking only when they needed to. They'd argued all the way back from the

Rum Line, but Stephen wouldn't budge. In the end, Colin had given up. Stephen was in charge of his own life, he told himself. If he was dead set on having it out with Melissa, let him. But nothing good would come of it.

When the load was secured, Colin went over the charts and checked the travel time. He wanted to arrive a little before midnight, so they waited another hour before leaving. They spent the time on the dock, reminiscing about childhood memories. Neither of them wanted to continue an argument that was obviously going nowhere.

When the time was right, Colin fired up the Lion engine, and *Pegasus* roared out to sea heading west for Florida.

The sun set, and they drove on into the night. The sky was overcast and moonless. They ran with the lights on until they reached the Rum Line. Then Colin switched them off and slowed the boat to quiet the engine a bit.

Stephen swept the horizon with binoculars, looking for lights or the outline of another rumrunner moving fast and dark.

What he spotted instead was something he hadn't seen before. He tapped Colin and handed him the binoculars. "Starboard quarter," he said. "What is that?"

Colin slowed the boat to harbor speed for a more stable view and scanned the sea with the binoculars. He picked out a deep orange glow in the distance. It wasn't a light. There was only one thing it could be.

"Fire," he said.

They traded a worried look, and Colin edged the throttle forward. It was a fishing boat, they discovered as they approached. From its design, it could have been the *Lenore*. The fire was burning through the superstructure, but the hull was still intact. Colin saw no movement.

"Ahoy!" he shouted, "Anybody aboard?"

There was no answer.

"Could be someone hurt in there," said Stephen.

Colin slowed *Pegasus* to a crawl and came along the stricken boat's port side. If she'd been carrying any cargo, it was gone now. Colin spotted what looked like freshly damaged wood along the gunwales and in the superstructure.

"Those what I think they are?" asked Stephen.

"Yeah," said Colin. "Bullet damage."

"Hold her steady," said Stephen. "I'll go over."

Colin eyed the rapidly spreading flames.

"Be quick," he said. "And take your pistol."

Stephen nodded and showed him the gun was already in his hand.

They gently bumped the burning boat, and Stephen leaped across. Colin could feel the heat from the flames. The fire would eventually burn the boat to the waterline, and what remained would sink.

Stephen found a piece of tarp and batted at the flames with it. He ducked into the burning deckhouse and out of sight. Colin's heart leapt, but a moment later, Stephen reappeared and gestured that he was coming back. Colin again edged up against the burning hull, and Stephen jumped back aboard.

"Nobody," Stephen said. "But there was blood. A lot of it. "

They were quiet for a moment, then Colin said, "we shouldn't be here."

"No," said Stephen. "Nothing we can do. Let's go."

Colin slid the throttle forward, and they left the burning hulk behind them.

"Deckhouse was shot to hell," Stephen said. "There were empty bottles. Figure they took the cargo, dumped the bodies overboard, and used some of the alcohol to get the fire going."

Colin nodded. The fire would be visible for miles. If the *Mojave* was out tonight, she'd surely come to investigate. That was reason enough to get far away. But there was another, more chilling reason. Someone had decided that piracy was easier than rumrunning. And someone else had paid with their life.

It was a bad omen. Part of Colin's mind was telling him to turn around and head home. But he pushed on into the darkness.

"Where do you want me drop you?" Colin asked as the lights of the shoreline came into view.

"Same place we landed that first time," said Stephen. "I'll walk in from there."

Colin nodded. "Take me a little under an hour to make the drop from there. Unload, get paid, call it two hours to get back. Maybe two and a half. That long enough for you?"

"It'll do," said Stephen.

"Wish you wouldn't do this," Colin said one last time as he steered around the south end of the barrier island. Ellis Kusack's palatial mansion was a huge pile of stone and scaffolding overlooking the sea.

"I have to," said Stephen.

Then there was nothing left to say.

STEPHEN WATCHED *Pegasus* motor slowly away, out of the mangroves and up the channel. When the boat was gone, he turned and made his way up toward the sandy road.

He was committed now.

The landscape was empty and still as Stephen trudged up the road toward Harmony Beach. He rehearsed what he would say to Melissa, considered what was too harsh and what she deserved. He reached the village and moved quietly past the houses and the darkened general store. He could hear the raucous music from the club now. The club seemed to be the only thing alive in Harmony Beach. Melissa would be there now, either in the back office or out on the floor.

When and where would she be by herself? He couldn't simply walk in and ask for her. He needed to slip in unseen and confront her someplace where they could be alone.

The bar was obviously out of the question, as was the store-room. There were usually a couple heavyset goons back there. They unloaded liquor on the docks, but Stephen suspected they also served as bouncers. He guessed they enjoyed that part more than unloading boats.

It would have to be the office but getting there unseen wouldn't be easy. As he reached the club, he left the sidewalk that led to the front doors and moved quietly through the parking lot, into the darkness at the end of the building. An armadillo scut-tled away from beneath the bushes near the wall. Stephen had been in the office once. There was a window that must look out on this side. He found it a few yards down and stepped through the bushes to peer inside. The office was dark and empty. He tested the window and found that it swung out from the bottom. A stick lay on the sill to prop it open.

He could get in well enough. But could he get out quickly if he needed to? For the first time, Stephen considered what might happen if this went wrong, if someone else came back to the office before Melissa and found him waiting. Then he heard voices from the parking lot, drunk and laughing. A car started up and rattled away. Someone might wander around the corner at any moment. They wouldn't be any happier to find him skulking around out here than inside.

That decided it. He lifted a leg onto the sill and carefully slid through into the office. He could feel the beat of the music vibrating through the wooden floor, could smell the beer and sweat. He moved carefully in the dim light until he found a small desk lamp and switched that on. Then he sat down behind the desk facing the door and waited.

It took about ten minutes for someone to come back to the office. Stephen heard footsteps and put his hand into his pocket, on the butt of his Colt Hammerless. Then the door opened, and he released the gun as he heard Melissa's voice call back to someone.

The door opened, and she jumped as she switched on the lights.

"Stephen! Jesus! You scared the hell out of me!"

"Hello, Melissa."

She looked back over her shoulder, then quickly closed the door. "You can't be here. If they find you…"

"I'll go," he said, "but not until we have a talk about your boss."

She stepped toward him, but the desk remained between them. "Look, I'll tell you whatever you want to know, but not here. I have a house in town. Go there and wait. I'll come after we close."

"No, it won't take that long. I already got the picture. I just want to hear you tell me why you let me think you wanted me."

"Oh, for God's sake, Stephen! Do you think I *want* to be Ellis's plaything? You think it's not humiliating every time he puts his arm around my ass and then sends me off to get the boys more cigars?"

She stepped around the desk toward him, and Stephen saw the pleading in her eyes. "Like I told you, Ellis wants what he sees, and he gets what he wants. He didn't ask what I want. I want *you*."

Then she was in his arms and kissing him, and for a moment there were no mobsters on the other side of the wall ready to kill him. There was no rumrunning, no family farm. There was nothing but the two of them, and Stephen knew she meant what she'd said.

"Ellis is away up north," she murmured when they finally broke the kiss. "He's away a lot. When he's gone, we can be together. But we've got to be careful."

Stephen shook his head. "I'm not going to share you with him."

"I don't have a choice! Don't you get it?" She looked nervously at the door. "You have to go before someone comes looking for me. My place. Take a left on Mason Street, and it's on the right. Look for the blue shutters."

Stephen hesitated, and she kissed him again. "I'll come later, I promise."

Then she hurried him to the window, and he climbed out, his mind a jumble of emotion.

He stood outside the window after she closed it. He watched her switch off the lights and leave.

He understood what it was like to be trapped in a situation you didn't want. That had been his life since his father died, and Colin fled to the army. And he knew he'd wanted her before, but could he still want her now, knowing what he knew?

What the hell was he going to do?

Whatever it was, he realized suddenly that he couldn't just go back to her house and wait. Colin would be heading back to pick him up. He checked his watch and decided he had a little time to spare, but not enough to wait for the club to close.

She'd be disappointed if he wasn't there, though. He had enough time to at least go by and leave her a note, so she wouldn't think he'd rejected her out of hand.

He composed it over and over again as he walked through the night toward the sleeping village. He would promise to come again at least. She deserved to be heard out, even if he couldn't deal with her affair with Kusack. If he couldn't, she should know that he understood, that he wasn't angry anymore.

Not at her anyway.

He found Mason Street easily enough. The town was tiny. The street signs were shiny and new. Stephen suspected the streets hadn't even had names before Ellis Kusack came along. He was still trying to word his note as he walked down the street and didn't pay attention to the sound of the car behind him. Someone heading home from the club.

But then a spotlight washed over him, and the car pulled up behind him. Stephen wheeled around in time to see the doors open. He saw the painted shield and the words, "Harmony Beach Sheriff's Department."

There were four of them. Healthy-looking young men in uniforms. The driver was the oldest; Stephen assumed he was the Sheriff.

"Good evening," the Sheriff said. "Your name wouldn't be Ridley, would it?"

Stephen said nothing. He looked around for an escape route, but the deputies were already circling to cut him off. On unfamiliar ground, in the dark, he didn't like his chances if he ran.

"I'm Sheriff Mayhew. Had a warning to be on the lookout for illegal liquor smugglers, and you sure look like the description."

"Heard that from Ellis Kusack, did you?"

The Sheriff grinned. "Got a call from a concerned citizen."

"So what happens now?" He looked around at the deputies.

"Supposed to be two of you," said the Sheriff. "Where's the other one?"

"Came alone this time."

"Well, then you'll have a nice fast boat somewhere nearby won't you? Have to check it for contraband."

Stephen sighed. This wasn't going to end well, but there was nothing left but to try. He spun on the ball of his foot and launched a punch at the nearest deputy. It caught him by surprise, and the deputy went down, stunned.

Stephen whirled to grapple with another one, but then there was the rush of air behind him, the impact of a nightstick, and Stephen fell, surrounded by angry faces.

Then the kicking began.

12

COLIN STEERED *PEGASUS* PAST THE MOTORBOAT CLUB, WHERE THE party was still in full swing, and headed down the channel between the barrier island and the mainland. He was still annoyed at Stephen for putting him into this situation, but at least the run had been a success. He'd reached the drop point with no trouble. The buyer's people had been waiting and were quick to unload his cargo and pay up. Colin was running slightly ahead of schedule, with a thick sheaf of bills in his shirt pocket. It could have been worse.

He slowed the boat and steered in toward the small, mangrove-choked inlet with the engine softly idling. He hoped Stephen had had it out with the woman from the bar and was done with it. He hoped he'd be ready to go home and put this place behind him.

But something wasn't right, he saw as he glided in between the trees. There were shapes waiting in the darkness, people.

He was about to throw the engine into reverse and back out when someone shouted, "That's right, that's right, bring her on in. Assuming you want your brother back, that is."

Flashlight beams speared out of the night, illuminating him

and *Pegasus*. Then one swept downward to reveal Stephen, lying in a battered heap at the feet of a man in a uniform. There were four of them, he saw now, all uniformed. The local law. Two had rifles leveled at him. There was nothing he could do, he realized. He was well and truly caught.

"Bring her up here nice and slow," shouted the one in charge. He must be the Sheriff. "Hands where I can see them."

Colin cut the engine and let *Pegasus* coast in until the hull ground gently against the sand.

"Stephen?" he called out, but Stephen lay still and only groaned.

"He'll be all right," said the Sheriff, "if you don't do anything stupid, that is. Step up here." He pointed to a spot nearby where the ground rose a bit.

"Arms out," the Sheriff added as Colin jumped down from the boat.

Colin stood where they told him to and held his arms out. One of the deputies quickly and expertly frisked him. First he found Colin's Bulldog revolver and held it up to show the Sheriff before tossing it to another deputy. Then he found the money in Colin's shirt pocket.

"Have a look here, Sheriff," he said, holding up the folded bills.

"Toss 'em over, Danny. Let's have a closer look."

The Sheriff snatched the bills out of the air, and they disappeared into his pocket. "Well, I'd say that's evidence of a crime. We'll confiscate that. What's in the boat?"

Colin said nothing. One of the deputies walked over to *Pegasus* and checked the interior with his flashlight.

"Empty, Sheriff."

Colin was looking at Stephen. He was a mess, covered in bruises and abrasions. His face was swollen. He managed to open his eyes and look up at Colin. "Hey," he said weakly.

"It's all right," Colin said. "I'll get you out of here." Then he turned to meet the Sheriff's eyes and fixed him with the cold stare he'd learned watching men in the trenches of France.

"You shouldn't have done that."

The Sheriff chuckled. "Well, your brother resisted arrest. You want to take a crack too, go right ahead."

The deputies laughed at that. Then the Sheriff shook his head. "You're not from around here, Mr. Ridley, so you won't know me. But this is my island."

"I thought it was Ellis Kusack's island."

The Sheriff's expression hardened a bit more. "Same thing. I know everything that goes on here. Don't think you can just come in here and do what you want. It looks like Mr. Kusack wasn't clear enough before, so I'll make it real simple. You're out of business. That means here, that means anywhere on the coast, that means selling on the Rum Line. You're done. If we see you again, here or anywhere else, if I so much as see you in church on Sunday morning, you'll be begging to get off with what your brother got. Is that clear enough?"

Colin said nothing until the Sheriff unsnapped his holster, took two surprisingly quick steps forward and jammed his pistol under Colin's chin.

"I said, is that clear enough?"

"Oh yeah," said Colin, "that's very clear."

"Good." The Sheriff stepped back and holstered his revolver. "Now get your brother and get the hell out of here."

Two deputies hauled Stephen to his feet. His hands were cuffed behind him and he couldn't stay on his feet. The deputies hauled him down to the boat, hefted him up and draped him over the bow. He lay there with his legs dangling in the shallow water.

"All right, go on," said the Sheriff.

Colin nodded toward the handcuffs. "You going to take those off him?"

The Sheriff sighed and dropped his hand to the butt of his

pistol again. "You got him back. You want to go home, or do you want to stay here?"

So no, they weren't. Colin put his arms around Stephen's legs and rolled him up onto the bow. Stephen groaned in pain. Then Colin jumped aboard and poled the boat back out of the mangroves. The Sheriff and his men disappeared into the night.

When he was safely out into the channel, Colin stowed the pole and hurried up to the foredeck. Stephen had managed to turn over and had nearly rolled off the side into the water. Colin helped him back to the cockpit and got him into a seat, his hands still cuffed awkwardly behind him.

"Think I screwed up," Stephen said, the words slurred through his swollen lips.

Colin nearly slapped him. "You're god damn right you screwed up! What the hell was this about, Stephen? You got yourself beat up. You got us robbed. You could have gotten us both killed! For what? For what?"

He turned away in disgust and started up the engine. Then he steered down the channel toward the gap that led out to sea. There was an open bottle of rum beneath the seat. He reached down and held it up to Stephen's mouth.

"Here. Rinse the blood out of your mouth."

Stephen did, wincing as the alcohol burned in his cuts and scrapes.

"Can you get these things off me?" he said at last.

"No, I can't get a pair of handcuffs off you here! We'll look for something when we get home."

He steered around the southern tip of the island, past Kusack's half-constructed palace. "All this for someone else's woman. That's rich. I thought you were smarter than that."

Stephen bristled. "Kusack's going to pay for this. He's going to pay."

Colin scoffed. "Yeah, how's that going so far?"

Stephen just repeated, "He's going to pay."

"Yeah, fine, tell yourself that. Just try to keep out of Mother's way for a few days. I don't want her to see you like this."

Colin slid the throttles forward and headed out to sea. "Then we're going to have a long talk about how all this works. Things are going to change, Stephen."

Stephen didn't answer. He turned in his seat and looked back at the lights of Kusack's mansion until they'd faded into the distance and were lost in the night.

By the time they reached Beckers Cay, nothing had changed. Colin shouted and swore. Stephen shifted painfully in the seat and complained that his shoulders hurt. But he never backed down.

A simple apology would have gone a long way, Colin thought to himself as they steered in toward the island's small anchorage. Stephen had done something headstrong and stupid, and they'd both paid the price. Now that the fear and the danger had faded, Colin could admit that Stephen had gotten the worst of it.

He looked over at his brother, glowering through his pain in the seat beside him. When they were growing up, Colin had been the one to rush into trouble while Stephen was always the good boy, the one his parents didn't need to worry about.

That had persisted right up until their father's death, and then Colin had done the ultimate rush into trouble and landed in the middle of the Great War. A lot of men just like him hadn't come back from France. Colin had, but he was changed by it. Everyone who came home was changed one way or another. Now Colin was the careful one, the one who looked for warning signs before rushing blindly into danger.

But there was more to it, he knew. He'd changed, but so had his brother. Surely Stephen hadn't been this unpredictable when they were boys? No, he was sure of it. He'd become more cautious, but Stephen had become more reckless as well. Had the pressure of running the farm by himself done that? Or had it always been there, tamped down by their father and overshadowed by his older brother's antics? He wasn't sure, but the change in Stephen worried him. Perhaps precisely because the war had shown him exactly what kind of horrible things could happen to people who took too many risks.

A figure stood on the dock as they approached, silhouetted by the rising sun. As they drew closer, Colin recognized Marcus waiting for them.

"What's he doing there?" said Stephen.

"Don't know," Colin answered, "but he'll be handy for getting you out. He'll have tools to get those cuffs off."

Colin cut the engine and let the boat glide in. He tossed the aft mooring line to Marcus and then went forward to tie off the other line.

"We had a situation," he called to Marcus. "Help me get Stephen up."

Together they took him by the arms and helped him climb out of the boat.

"It's not as bad as it looks," said Colin.

Stephen grunted. "Yes, it is."

"We'll need some tools," Colin went on. "Hacksaw. Some snips maybe. Going to be a pain in the ass…"

He trailed off as he saw Marcus' stricken expression, and a chill fell over him. "What? What is it?"

"My Ada went to bring her some tea and tell her you two weren't back yet. She always wanted to hear as soon as someone saw the boat coming back."

"No," said Stephen. "No, no."

"It happened in her sleep," Marcus said. "I came up. She looks peaceful. It was peaceful."

Marcus looked down at his feet. "She's gone. Your mother's gone."

13

EMILY RIDLEY HAD BEEN A WELL-KNOWN AND RESPECTED FIGURE IN the local islands. Her funeral turned into a major event. They'd waited three days for the news to get around, and for Stephen to recover and be as presentable as possible.

When the day came, everyone on Beckers Cay was there, and boats showed up by the dozens from as far as Grand Bahama itself. There were far too many for Bishop Deveaux's little church, so they held the service in the front yard of the main house. Colin and Stephen stood side by side in front of her coffin as friends spoke about her. There were stories that even Colin didn't know. Then Colin spoke for the family. He'd thought Stephen should do it, but Stephen refused, saying he didn't trust himself to carry it off.

Colin spoke of Emily as a mother raising two sons in a new land, far from the civilized comforts of England. It had been a hard job, he said, in hard times, but they'd never quite realized how hard the family's struggles had been because their mother made everything seem so easy. He concluded by saying he hoped he and Stephen had learned how to claim that kind of strength for themselves as they went on without her.

Bishop Deveaux led a hymn, and then the long procession snaked up the hill to the family burial plot. They buried Emily beside her husband, Charles. A stone had been ordered from Nassau, but wouldn't arrive for several more days. Colin and Stephen stood beside the grave in silence as friends and farm workers paid their respects.

Finally, it was back down to the house where the women had laid out food, and people stood talking in small groups. The funeral had brought together people who hadn't seen each other in years. Like any funeral, it was as much a social occasion as a grieving ceremony.

Colin and Stephen shook hands, accepted condolences and embraces, and thanked people for coming. It was nearly sunset when the last boat departed from the inlet and the work of cleaning up could begin. By the time the last of the local women had been thanked for their help, had said once more how loved Emily was, and had gone home, it was nearly midnight.

Both the brothers were exhausted. Colin poured them a couple shots, and they settled into chairs in the parlor. Colin looked around the room and shook his head. The place looked much better than it had the night Marcus had brought him home from Nassau. Furniture had been replaced, and a new rug replaced the threadbare one that had been on the floor. The whole house had gained a new lease on life. It looked once more like the home of a prosperous island farmer even though the money had come from a very different place.

Emily was the reason for that. They'd done all this for her, and now she was gone.

"What do we do now?" he asked, to himself as much as to Stephen.

"Get some sleep," said Stephen. "I'm exhausted. Then...how long's it been since someone went to Big Spring? Simon will have a couple loads backed up by now."

"It's okay," said Colin. "I'll talk to Marcus tomorrow, have him start taking down the loading ramp. Don't worry about Simon. He'll find another buyer."

"What do mean another buyer? We're the buyer. What's wrong with the ramps?"

Colin sat up and looked across at Stephen. He could still see a bit of bruising around his eyes, and he'd noticed at the reception that Stephen still moved with a bit of stiffness left over from his beating.

"You want to keep going?" he asked, incredulous. "Keep running booze?"

Stephen looked just as confused. "Of course. Why wouldn't we?"

"Well, what's the point? We did it to take care of mother. Pay off the creditors. Fix up the house so she'd be comfortable here. What's it for now?"

"It's for the money."

"Stephen, we were stuck here for mother's sake. You more than me, I know. You don't want to stay here and run the farm. I sure don't want it. It's time to shut it down. Take the money we've got so far, sell the land, and we'll have a good stake. It's time to move on. Live our own lives."

"Live your own life. You mean give up and slink away somewhere, don't you?" Stephen shook his head in disgust. "That's what you do, isn't it?"

"Hey!"

"It's what you do. You know it. You sneaked off to join the Army, you—"

"I did what I thought I had to do."

Stephen scoffed. "Oh, don't act like the war was some great sacrifice you made. You wanted it! You ran to it!"

Colin didn't have an answer. Stephen was right about that. He'd run away to the war to escape Beckers Cay. He went expecting adventure and glory, but that wasn't what he found. Just because he'd walked into that slaughterhouse willingly didn't mean he wasn't surprised by what he saw there. He still carried the experience with him. He'd take it back if he could. But how could he make Stephen understand that?

"We're not going anywhere!" Stephen had stood up now and was pacing between their chairs, full of nervous energy. "We're going to keep running because that's what I want to do. You got your turn. You went off to war. You came back and you got to be a playboy gambler in Nassau. You always did just what you wanted, and all the while you let me scratch in the dirt growing rope fibers that nobody wants."

"Stephen."

"We had to drag you home when mother had the stroke, and just like that you're the golden boy? I know what to do! We'll run booze into Florida! Well all right, I did that too. And you know what? I like it? I like how it makes me feel. And I really like the money. I'm not quitting just because you think you've done enough."

"What do you mean, enough?"

"You thought, all right, I'll save the farm. I guess I owe them that much. But now she's dead you figure you're off the hook. Well you're not, Colin! You're not. You still owe me!"

"Enough!" Colin roared, rising quickly to his feet. "You're right. I ran away from here, and I left you to take over the farm. You're right. I did that."

"You're damn right you did."

"And I'm sorry. I can't change that now. All I can do now is make sure you're okay. That's what she told me to do. The farm's a dead end. She knew it. We all knew it. But you didn't have anything else. What were you going to do when she was gone?"

Stephen was looking at him in amazement, struggling to process his emotions.

"If I could have taken you both back to Nassau, I'd have come up with something else. But here? There's not a lot of ways to make money out here. I came up with one. But it's not a good one."

He forced his voice lower, took a breath. "It was easy money, but it's no game. It's dangerous out there. People get killed. They get dumped at sea, their boats burned, and nobody knows what happened to them. They just go out one time too many, and they don't come back. We pushed our luck far enough."

"What about Melissa?"

"What about her?" Colin felt his anger rising again. God, Stephen could be so stupid when he set his mind to it. "What about her? She's Kusack's woman, Stephen! Not yours! You already got yourself beaten half to death over her. For nothing!"

"I know who beat me up! I was there, remember? I know their faces. I know their names. I know who sent them. They're going to pay for that."

"Jesus, will you listen to yourself? You can't go toe to toe with Ellis Kusack. You'll end up just like the crew of that boat."

Stephen poured himself another drink and knocked it back. He looked out the window into the night. "You know what running this damn farm for all those years did to me? It made me tough. I bet you don't believe that. I bet you think you're the tough one because you went to war, and you stared death in the face. But I'm tough too. Maybe not the way you are, but tough."

"I know it," Colin said softly, but Stephen went on as if he hadn't heard.

"I'm not going to back down," he said. "I didn't let father break me, I didn't let you or this farm break me, and I'm not going to stand for getting kicked around by Ellis Kusack. I'm going to run into Florida and make money, and I'm going to keep my eyes open. And when the time's right, I'm going to make him pay."

Then Stephen turned from the window to face him, and Colin saw the determination. He saw that he wasn't going to talk Stephen out of this. "That's with you or without," Stephen said. "If you want to watch my back, then you're welcome to come.

You've got a good boat. But if you don't, I'm going anyway. I'll run the *Lenore* into Florida if I have to. You let me know what you decide. I'm going to get some sleep."

He set down his empty glass, walked past Colin, and headed for the stairs.

"Stephen."

His voice was calm, quiet. Stephen stopped and turned around.

"All right," said Colin. "I don't want to bring in any more from Simon. But we've got a few weeks' worth of runs in the sheds already. We'll run them in and see what happens."

Stephen gave him a long look, then finally nodded. "Okay," he said. "We can figure it out in the morning."

Then he was gone, the stairs creaking as he headed up to his room. Colin let out a sigh and settled back into a chair.

What else could he have done? He knew Stephen wasn't bluffing about going it alone if he had to. Colin couldn't let him do that. Something had happened to his brother. He had all the energy and misdirected anger Colin recognized in his own younger self. He was impulsive, reckless, and proud. And he had a short fuse. The war had taught Colin how to rein in those impulses. It had taught him how to survive. But that was something Stephen hadn't learned. Here, struggling all day with the doomed farm, he'd never had a chance to test himself. Now he'd taken on more than he could handle, and he didn't know enough to realize it.

Colin didn't know how he was going to shift Stephen off the path he was set on. But he could hardly let him go on alone. If he did that, there wasn't a doubt in his mind that Stephen was going to get himself killed.

14

THEY WAITED A FEW MORE DAYS, BOTH TO GRIEVE AND TO LET Stephen recover. Then they resumed making runs to the Rum Line in *Lenore*. While Colin handled the wholesaling of their cargos aboard one freighter or another, Stephen began looking for buyers who needed cargo delivered ashore.

That was where the real money was, Stephen told himself, in putting everything on the line to run a cargo past the Coast Guard and get away clean. But inside, he had to admit that wasn't the real attraction. The money from wholesaling was more than enough to meet his needs. All but one.

Stephen had discovered that he needed to run. He needed the thrill and the danger. Even seeing what the pirates had done to a runner and his boat hadn't been enough to scare him off.

This wasn't like him, he thought, sitting at a barrel table waiting for a contact to return with his deposit money. He'd led a quiet farmer's life. He'd been the good son, the one his parents didn't have to worry about. The one who stayed and worked to save the family after Colin ran off for adventure. It occurred to him now to wonder if that had been wrong all along. Had Colin just made him look mild by comparison? Or had this experience changed him the way the war had changed his brother?

In the end, it didn't matter. Whatever the cause, he was a rumrunner now, and Stephen didn't think he could ever be a struggling farmer again.

The buyer reappeared through the hatch at the far end of the hold. He worked a speakeasy in Miami, and their current supplier was watering down the product too much. Stephen had reassured him that theirs was the genuine article. Real rum from the islands. And they didn't cut it at all.

"Are we good?" Stephen asked as the man sat down across the table from him. He gathered there was a partner on his boat who held the money and who had to agree.

"We're good," the buyer said. He slid the money across the table, and Stephen quickly pocketed it. The buyer unfolded a map and pointed out a spot in a marshy wetland behind the barrier islands.

"Drop-off's here. You can cut through here. Or here." He pointed out inlets through the barrier islands.

"No problem," said Stephen. "Eleven tomorrow night, right?"

"That's right."

"Okay," said Stephen. "Then we're done. See you tomorrow."

COLIN STOOD AT THE RAIL, watching the busy flotilla of runners moving among the freighters like bees through a stand of flowers. He wasn't happy to be here again, though he admitted to himself that he had nowhere else to be. What if Stephen hadn't gotten drunk on danger? If he'd agreed to sell the farm and start somewhere else? What would he have done? He'd been bluffing that night. He had no idea where they would have gone, what that "new start" he'd promised would have looked like.

Until he had a better answer, all he could do was let Stephen have his way and try to protect him from whatever danger he got them into.

He looked up and was startled to see a new boat approaching. At first he thought it was a Coast Guard cutter, finally coming over the line to clear them out. But the newcomer wasn't quite that big. It was a motor yacht, and a huge one. Its white hull gleamed in the sun, and Colin could make out uniformed crewmen on the foredeck.

It turned to drop anchor, and Colin saw the name *Fianna* on the stern. He watched, and it soon became clear that they weren't sending a boat over to the freighters to buy. Smaller boats were coming to them, loaded with cargo.

"Who's that?" he asked a passing sailor.

"*Fianna*? Showed up a couple days ago. Belongs to some big wheel from up north. They say he just took delivery and sailed her down here. Docks in some little burg called Harmony Beach."

Kusack. Colin thanked the sailor and turned back to the rail. So Kusack had gotten himself a cruiser. He could run his own liquor now. Something that size could carry enough booze to keep the Motorboat Club stocked for weeks, assuming he could get past the Coast Guard. It would be hard not to notice. Either she was fast for her size, or Kusack had managed to bribe someone into looking the other way.

Stephen appeared and leaned against the rail at his side. "Whoa. Who's that?"

Colin took a breath. "They say it's Kusack's boat." He felt Stephen stiffen beside him.

"Is he aboard?"

"I don't know. What does it matter?"

But he knew. Stephen was imagining a luxurious stateroom, and Melissa waiting in Kusack's bed.

Stephen turned and leaned his back against the rail. "It doesn't," he said. "Deal's set. We go in tomorrow night. *Lenore's* unloaded. Let's get the hell out of here."

~

COLIN SPENT THE DAY TUNING *PEGASUS'* engine and cleaning the hull. It had been a while since they'd taken her on a run, and he wanted to be sure she was in prime shape.

At noon, a packet boat arrived carrying Emily's gravestone. Along with some of the farmworkers, they carried it up the hill to the small plot and carefully planted the stone in the ground beside their father's. They both stood quietly at the graves for a long time, lost in their own separate thoughts. Finally they walked back down the hill.

Over a light dinner, they went over the charts and plotted their course. This was their first time making this drop, and Colin wanted to be sure of his approach.

Then it was time to leave. *Pegasus* was loaded, fueled, and ready. Colin climbed into the cockpit and looked up at his brother, still on the dock bidding Marcus goodbye. Stephen was smiling, almost bouncing on the balls of his feet. He was happier than Colin had seen him since the funeral.

Stephen needed this, he realized. He'd gotten hooked on it, just like men in the trenches had gotten hooked on black-market morphine. Those stories hadn't ended well.

Then Stephen climbed down into the cockpit beside him. "Good to go," he said.

Colin nodded and started the engine. They pulled away from the dock and headed out toward the Florida Strait.

The crossing was straightforward. The weather was calm, but heavy cloud began rolling in from the west and obscured the moon and stars. Colin needed a flashlight to check his chart. He kept *Pegasus'* lights on until they approached the Rum Line. They knew they were close because they passed to the south of the informal flotilla of rumrunners, close enough to make out the lights in the distance. Then Colin took *Pegasus* dark, and he steered a bearing toward the coast that would take them to one of the two possible channels through the barrier islands.

They were in United States waters, not quite halfway to the coast, when Colin realized they weren't alone. He saw a tiny flicker of light off the port side. It appeared suddenly, burned white for maybe thirty seconds, then vanished. It wasn't a running light. He didn't know what it was. He tapped Stephen's shoulder and pointed it out to him a few seconds before it vanished.

"What is it?" Stephen asked.

Colin shrugged and slowed the throttle. "Don't know. Got to be a boat. Not running any lights though. Another runner?"

He cut the throttle further. *Pegasus* slowed to idle, and now he could hear the sound of engines across the water. The other boat was running dark and fast, coming closer.

"Not the Coast Guard," said Stephen.

That was obvious enough. The question was, was this another runner minding his own business, or something else? Colin remembered the bullet-ridden burning boat.

He strained to make out the other boat's course from the sound of its engines. It sounded like it was racing at top speed.

"There!" said Stephen, and now Colin could make out a darker shape coming toward them. It was big. Huge to be moving that fast. It was almost on a collision course, the hull now a ghostly white.

Colin slammed the throttles full open, and *Pegasus* took off like a kicked mule, cutting across the other ship's path as it approached. They crossed perhaps a hundred yards in front of her, and then the night lit up with the harsh beams of spotlights. This was followed almost immediately by a sound Colin had thought he'd never hear again: the roar of heavy machine guns.

"Down!" he shouted, and he threw the wheel hard to port to steer out of their line of fire. He looked back and saw bullets churning the surface in their wake. *Pegasus* sped past the other boat, and now they were close enough to get a clear look at her.

"It's the god damn *Fianna*!" Colin yelled. Kusack's people were making good on their threat.

"Son of a bitch!" Stephen snapped.

The machine gun fire had stopped now. The guns were probably set up on portable tripods at the bow, and Colin's maneuver had taken them out of their field of fire. But as they passed, Colin saw movement on the deck. A sailor ran to the rail and opened up with what looked like a Thompson gun. Colin saw the muzzle flashes and heard bullets slam into *Pegasus'* woodwork. Another light came on atop the superstructure and pinned them like a butterfly to a card, following them as they moved.

"What the hell do we do?" said Stephen.

"We run!" It wasn't as if they could take on the *Fianna* in some kind of battle at sea. They didn't even have their pistols since their encounter with Sheriff Mayhew. Their only hope was to outrun her.

But God, she was fast! Colin saw her wheeling hard to port to follow them, her wake carving a wide arc through the sea. He had no idea what kind of power she must be putting out to make that speed. Hopefully *Pegasus* was even faster.

Colin cut to starboard and then back to port again, hoping to lose the spotlight. But it was no good. He tried something desperate, sweeping back around to cross *Fianna's* bow in the opposite direction of her turn. It would mean running under the guns again, but if they could take them by surprise and get through, *Fianna* would be turning away from them. It would take her time to reverse and turn back. Colin could use that time to open up some distance, lose them in the night.

"Stay down," he shouted as he yanked the wheel around. Whoever was manning the spotlight wasn't expecting that move and lost them. In the darkness, Colin gave *Pegasus* every bit of speed she had and raced across *Fianna's* bow.

The machine guns opened up, and Colin saw tracer rounds lancing into the sea nearby. Then bullets were slamming into the hull. He saw wood splintering around him, but all he could do was duck and hope their speed would carry them through. He hunkered down in the cockpit and waited for the hot impact of a bullet.

It never came. The gunfire stopped, and they were clear. Behind him, Colin could see *Fianna* still turning away from them.

"Are you all right?" he shouted at Stephen.

"Yeah!" Stephen answered, "but they've hit the engine!"

He was right, Colin realized. The Lion engine was sputtering, and their speed had dropped. Even with the throttle fully open, they were barely making half the speed they should have made. Colin steered away from *Fianna* and studied his gauges. Oil pressure was holding. The water temperature was a little hot, but that was to be expected given how they'd been running. He listened to the engine and decided that at least a couple of cylinders were down. The gunfire must have blown some valves. She'd be leaking fuel, but not enough to worry about right now. But she was straining to keep working at full load. If he wasn't careful, the engine could go completely.

"Damn it," he muttered. Behind him, *Fianna* had disappeared into the night, but he could hear her and knew Kusack's men were still looking for them.

Colin did the only thing he could think of. He cut the engine completely, and *Pegasus* came to a stop. It felt suddenly incongruous, bobbing gently in the dark.

"What are we doing?" Stephen asked, and now Colin could hear the fear in his voice.

"Dump the cargo," he said.

"Dump it? What? Overboard? What about—"

"It's heavy," Colin said. "Right now, we need all the speed we can get. I'll see to the engine. Go!"

Stephen climbed out of the cockpit and went forward. Colin

opened the fairing and was assaulted by the smell of petrol and burning oil. He played his flashlight across the engine and could see where bullets had scarred the block. They'd come through the top deck, torn off most of one of the valve covers and damaged one of the overhead camshafts on the port side. The starboard side was undamaged at least. But three cylinders on the port side were out of commission, venting fluids through the valves and creating a fire hazard. He wouldn't be able to fix it here. He could see that much.

Colin stretched forward to close the cutoff valves that shut off fuel to the engine's port side. He wasn't convinced that the remaining cylinders were doing them any good with that damaged camshaft. And the last thing he needed was petrol mist spraying over the hot engine and setting her on fire. They'd have to make the best speed they could on just six cylinders. *Pegasus* was crippled. And *Fianna* was damned fast. He wasn't even sure they could outrun her in this condition.

He could hear her engines in the distance, punctuated by splashes as Stephen tossed burlocks overboard. He'd done all he could here, so he switched off the light and closed the fairing. Looking astern, he could see *Fianna's* searchlights probing the dark water, drawing closer.

Stephen came back and dropped into the cockpit beside him. "Well, that's another load wasted," he said glumly. "At least someone got to drink the last one."

Colin was more concerned with getting them out of this alive. He carefully started the engine, kept it running at idle, and listened to the remaining cylinders sputter. There was some vibration in the drive shaft. The Lion wasn't meant to run just one side. But it would have to do. The lights were coming closer, nearly on them now.

Colin edged the throttles forward and turned carefully to port. She at least felt more responsive now, with the cargo gone. But then a light veered across their wake, and one of the machine guns opened up again. He threw the throttle open and turned sharply away from it.

But *Fianna* had scented her prey now. Even without a light on them, the guns started laying down fire around them. Colin saw tracers drill by them in the darkness. A lucky shot could kill them at any moment.

Pegasus was at full speed but as Colin feared, she couldn't outrun *Fianna* on her damaged engine. *Fianna* was bearing down on them from astern, filling the water around them with bullets. A light swept across them and held this time. Colin veered around, throwing himself and Stephen hard against the bulkhead. Speed was no use now. All that remained was maneuverability.

Then the guns fell silent again. Colin looked up from the controls and saw that *Fianna* was breaking off, making full speed away from them.

"They're running!" Stephen said. "What happened?"

Colin pointed off to starboard where lights were approaching. Then an amplified voice boomed across the water.

"Small craft, this is the Coast Guard cutter *Mojave*. Heave to and stand by to be boarded."

Colin put his forehead down on the cockpit fairing and laughed. He couldn't stop laughing. The bloody Coast Guard had saved their lives!

He looked up into Stephen's incredulous face and pointed toward the empty space where their cargo had been. He reached down beneath the seat and found the one remaining half-empty bottle of rum aboard. He flipped it overboard, and then Stephen was laughing too.

"We're just innocent pleasure boaters!" Colin said with some difficulty as tears of laughter rolled down his face.

"Out for a midnight cruise!" Stephen agreed.

"Thank you, oh, thank you for saving us, brave Coast Guardsmen!"

They managed to get themselves under control as the *Mojave* lowered a boat. The cutter instructed them to shut down their engine and stand up in the cockpit. They kept their hands visible, and Stephen waved a greeting as the boat approached and played a bright, handheld light across *Pegasus*.

"Well, you're shot to hell," said a voice from behind the glare. "Guess we'll need to get you two aboard and take her in tow."

Colin had heard that voice before. Then the light shifted, and he saw himself looking into the grinning face of Sam Blake.

15

"So you've probably figured out I'm not really a rumrunner," said Blake as he sat down across from them.

They were in a cabin aboard the *Mojave*. It wasn't quite a cell, but they'd been told to stay there, and a guard stood outside the door. The cutter's Medical Officer had confirmed that they were unhurt, and the crew had quickly and effectively gotten *Pegasus* under tow. Now they were underway, presumably toward the Coast Guard station in Miami.

"My name really is Sam Blake," he said. "Lieutenant Sam Blake. I'm assigned to work intelligence on the Rum Line. Collecting evidence, steering runners toward the *Mojave* where I can. Trying to shut that operation down and put the bad guys in jail."

Stephen gave Colin a concerned look, but Blake waved it off.

"Ah, don't worry," he said. "I can't prove what I know you're doing. This is the first time I've seen you in American waters, and you're clean." He scoffed. "Looks like you boys have got a lot bigger problems than me."

"That's why you tipped us to Harmony Beach," said Colin. "You were sending us to the *Mojave*."

"That's right," Blake admitted. "But you slipped the trap." He shrugged. "It was a good plan anyway. How we caught Kusack's last guy."

"So we're not under arrest?" Stephen asked.

Blake shook his head. "Like I said, I got nothing on you that will stick in court. Far as the Coast Guard's officially concerned, you're a pair of innocent boatmen in the wrong place at the wrong time. It happens. All these gangsters running around the sea."

"So what happens now?"

"You'll be put ashore at Miami. We'll do what we can to get your boat seaworthy for the trip home. But before that happens, I want to have a talk with you. I could use your help."

Colin didn't like the sound of that. "How's that?"

Blake chuckled. "You've been out there. You know how hard it is running you guys down. For every load we stop, a dozen get through. Even when we do get one, it doesn't matter. We nailed Kusack's last guy. He just went out and got you. It's a bum game."

He stopped for a moment and shook his head. "Look, I got nothing against a good drink. The law's the law, and it's my job to enforce it. But there's a lot worse things out there than a guy keeping a roof over his family by running booze."

"Things like Ellis Kusack," Colin offered.

Blake nodded. "That's right. Like him. I can do a lot more good taking him down than picking off a runner every couple days. And it looks like you've got a pretty big problem with him too."

"You could say that," said Stephen. Stephen sat back in his chair, arms crossed. He glared across the table at Blake, and Colin silently urged him to just shut up before he got them in deeper than they already were.

"I don't know how it happened," Blake continued. "Doesn't matter. But you two sure got on his bad side, and that's no place you want to be. I got a file on him from up north. He's nasty business. If he doesn't like someone, they tend not to be around very long. You got lucky tonight. Next time..."

Blake let it hang there, looking Colin in the eye.

"So what do you want from us?" Colin asked.

"I want you to testify against him, of course," said Blake. "You two know how his operation works. You were there. You can name names, places, dates. You're not all we got on him, but you could be what seals it. You'll get full immunity for cooperating. Hell, I'll claim you were working undercover for me the whole time if that helps."

Colin raised an eyebrow. "And we get..."

"You get clear!" said Blake. "You get a clean slate with us, and more important, you put Kusack away before your luck runs out."

Colin sat back and thought about it. He wasn't convinced that the deal was the sure thing Blake was trying to paint it as. He didn't want to trust his life to American cops and courts. Kusack was clever and slippery, and he had the resources to bring in the best lawyers, or to simply bribe whomever needed bribing. It was a long way from certain that he'd go down.

Kusack's crew hadn't been looking for them tonight; they just stumbled across him and Stephen, so they took their shot. Right now Kusack didn't like them, but Colin doubted he cared enough to come looking for them if they stayed out of his way. But if they testified against him in court, and he didn't go down hard...that would be another story. It wouldn't be sailors next time but professional mob killers. Even if Kusack did go to prison, there would be someone else to take his place. They might find themselves hunted anyway. He couldn't see where Blake was risking anything in this deal. But he and Stephen were risking their lives.

No, it was a bad deal, and Colin wasn't about to get the two of them in any deeper. He was about to tell Blake so when Stephen cut him off.

"No deal, Blake," Stephen said, leaning forward and fixing Blake with a hard stare. "I'll deal with Kusack my own way." .

Colin looked at his brother in amazement, and Blake's jaw hung open in frank disbelief.

"You'll what?"

"I said I'll deal with him. Thanks for your help. But we're not going to testify."

"How, exactly, do you plan to 'deal with him?'" Blake asked, and Stephen was about to answer, but Colin kicked Stephen's foot under the table and cut him off.

"My brother's upset," he said. "We could have died out there tonight."

Blake shook his head. "Look, you two seem like decent enough guys. I know you just got into this because you figured it would be easy money, and maybe you needed that. But if you're going on some kind of personal vendetta against Ellis Kusack... trust me, you're in over your heads."

"You don't have to worry about us," said Stephen, and again Colin kicked him in the ankle.

"He's serious business, son. He's not some bully with a glass jaw that's going to break as soon as you stand up to him. He's connected. We're talking mobster connected."

"Which is why we're not going to testify," said Colin.

"Okay, yeah, I get that. But if you think you're going to take him on yourselves, that's just dumb. He'll come at you while you're looking the other way, and he'll burn down everything you've got and bury your bodies at sea. He's done it before."

Colin put his palms down on the table. "All right," he said. "My brother's upset, but we're not suicidal. We get it. Thanks for your help, Lieutenant. Under the circumstances, I'm glad you showed up when you did. But that doesn't mean we're going to testify for you. The answer's no."

Blake nodded. "All right," he said. "I tried. You two can rest here. We'll be in Miami in a few hours. If you change your mind, let me know."

Then Blake turned to Colin. "Can we talk outside for a minute?"

Colin glanced over at Stephen. "Whatever it is, you can say it in front of my brother."

Blake scoffed. "All right then." He took a breath. "I was going to say, keep an eye on your brother. I think he's going over the edge. If you're not careful, he's going to get himself in hot water real fast."

"I've got his back," said Colin. "He'll be all right."

Blake nodded. "All right. Good luck to you."

When Blake was gone, Colin turned to Stephen and hissed, "What the hell is wrong with you?"

Stephen started to argue, but Colin nodded toward the door, where he assumed there was still a guard to overhear them.

"He tried to kill us tonight!" Stephen whispered. "Kusack's a mad dog. You don't just let a mad dog come at you. You put him down."

"Will you listen to yourself?" Colin started to go on, but then just shook his head and turned away. "Not here. Later. Damn it!"

He went to the cabin's porthole and behind him he heard Stephen huff and sit back down in his chair. Colin looked out at the approaching lights of Miami. Everything was coming apart around him. Stephen was running amok, and he was no longer sure he could save him from himself.

One thing was certain though. Their rumrunning days were over.

THE NEXT DAY, under the Miami sun, Colin had a chance to look over the damage to his boat. *Pegasus* had definitely looked better.

Bullets had chewed at the polished teak woodwork, leaving splinters and ragged holes in the upper deck and long gashes in the hull. But it could have been much worse. Nothing was below the waterline. The boat was still seaworthy, just not as attractive as she had been.

The engine was another matter. As Colin had thought from his hurried inspection by flashlight, she needed a new valve cover, new camshafts, and a few other small parts. Otherwise, the engine seemed fine. Replace those parts, and she'd be good as new. But they wouldn't be easy to locate. The ideal solution would be to order them from the builder. But D. Napier and Sons were located in Acton, in West London. It would take weeks, months more likely, to get parts shipped across the Atlantic.

Colin knew he would order them anyway, but for the time being he needed replacements machined locally. That would be easier here than anywhere near Beckers Cay. So he and Stephen settled into a local hotel. They sent a telegram home to reassure Marcus and tell him they'd be delayed.

Then Colin found a machine shop that could build the parts he needed. The woodwork was less critical. He'd get to it when he could.

It took five days to get the engine back into good working order. The machinist did a fine job, Colin thought. He'd still replace the new parts with factory originals when they arrived. But these would do for now.

By the morning of their sixth day in Miami, *Pegasus* was, if not quite as good as new, good enough to make the journey home.

But Colin wasn't especially relieved as they crossed the straits back toward the Bahamas and Beckers Cay. He was more worried about Stephen than ever. After their nearly fatal encounter with Kusack's private navy, he knew he was finished with running. It was too dangerous. Blake had been right when he said they'd gotten very lucky. If the *Mojave* hadn't come along when she did, they most likely would have died out there. If you owe your life to the Coast Guard showing up, he thought, then rumrunning isn't the right line of work for you.

But he doubted Stephen would see it that way. His brother's anger was plainly visible, bubbling beneath the surface, waiting to erupt. Colin knew he was mired in his fantasy of revenge on Kusack. No doubt the next step was saving Melissa and riding away into the sunset like some dime novel cowboy hero. They'd avoided the subject in Miami, where they could focus instead on repairing *Pegasus* and getting home. But as the island appeared on the horizon, Colin knew they couldn't avoid it much longer.

They managed it long enough to dock and be welcomed home by Marcus and a group of worried workers. There was much shaking of heads and clucking over the damage to *Pegasus*, and thanks that they'd been delivered from danger. They managed to avoid it long enough to get back to the house and make themselves lunch.

But then Colin couldn't see any way to avoid it any longer.

"Guess we need to talk," he said over the scarred wooden work table in the kitchen.

"Guess so," said Stephen.

"I don't see any way to say it but to just come out and say it." Colin let out a long breath. "It's over, Stephen. We're done. You need to walk away from this."

"You know I'm not going to do that."

Colin knew he had to try. "Damn it, Stephen, what's it going to take? If that didn't convince you—"

"That's why we can't back down!" Stephen nearly shouted. "That son of a bitch tried to kill us. People like that don't stop. He'll keep at it until he gets us unless we make him stop."

"That's nonsense. He's not going to chase us down to the ends of the Earth. He doesn't care that much. He goes after us when we get in his way. So we get out of his way."

Stephen shook his head in disgust. "What happened to you

131

over there?" he asked. "Did you get shell shocked? What turned you into such a coward?"

Colin sat stunned for a long moment. Even Stephen seemed to realize he'd gone too far.

"I went off and left you here to deal with all of it," Colin said, slowly and quietly. "I did that, and you can hold that over me if you want. Beat me with it until you're satisfied. I earned that. But don't you ever call me a coward again, or I'll put your ass on the floor. You have no idea what I saw over there, and I hope you never do. But I walked straight into it with my eyes open."

"Yeah," said Stephen, "yeah. I know."

"And I'm not stupid, Stephen. I know what this is really about. It's about his woman."

"Melissa."

"Whatever. This is all about her. You want her, and he's got her. Pure and simple. It's a sucker play, kid. Sure she wanted you, as a plaything on the side."

Stephen turned away from the table and paced across the kitchen. "Go after me if you want, Colin. Not her."

"But she's what it's all about! Don't you get it? She wanted you that much, but not as much as Kusack's money, and his big house, and his fancy boat, and all the things he can give her. "

"Colin, I mean it."

"So do I, Stephen. You need to forget about her. There's plenty of good women out there. Don't get yourself killed taking on someone you can't handle over a woman who's made it damn clear that she's not good enough for you!"

Stephen whirled and flew at him. Colin saw it coming. Stephen's punch was telegraphed from the moment he turned. But Colin didn't use the counter moves they'd drilled into him. He let the punch through and cocked his head to one side, felt it graze his jaw and knock him back. He caught Stephen as he fell back, and they tumbled to the floor. Stephen threw his fists in a wild, unschooled flurry that broke uselessly on Colin like a wave against rocks.

When he sensed most of Stephen's energy was spent, he rolled to the side and pushed Stephen down to the floor. He pinned his brother's arms to his side. Stephen looked up at him, tears of rage in his eyes.

"You want to know what it's about?" Stephen said. He struggled against Colin's grip as if he was expected to but knew he couldn't break free.

"It's about me having one thing in my life that's really mine. I let this place take from me. And Father. And you. Now I've got nothing left. And I found something on my own, and I'll be damned if I let that cheap crook take from me too."

"You have to pick your battles, Stephen. I know it hurts. But I don't want to bury you. I'm done. I let you talk me into keeping on before. Not this time. *Pegasus* isn't going back out. It's finished."

Gradually, Stephen's struggles faded, and Colin let him up. Stephen sat back against the kitchen cabinets while Colin poured them a couple of drinks. They sat beside each other on the floor in silence as the sunlight from the window gradually slid across the floor and up the far wall.

That night, Colin heard the stairs creak as Stephen went down. It was after midnight. For a moment he considered getting up and going out. But no. He'd done all he could. Stephen had to find his own way. He heard the door open and close.

The next morning, one of the fishing boats was gone from the dock.

16

STEPHEN ARRIVED AT THE RUM LINE A HALF HOUR BEFORE SUNSET. It always seemed to be sunset here, the party always just taking off. He took the fishing boat slowly among the freighters as voices and the jangling sounds of dance music drifted down from their decks. He steered carefully through the smaller boats until he found the freighter he was looking for.

The *Edmund Kitts* was a relatively modern tramp steamer flying the American flag. She had a staircase lowered down the side of the hull and a line of floats for boats to tie off to. Stephen made his way to the deck, past stacked crates and incurious sailors, and entered the aft deckhouse. He followed a hand-lettered sign reading "Guest Cabins" down into the maze of the ship's crew area.

The sounds were different here. Laughter and moans punctuated the smells of sex. As he passed one door he heard the smack of flesh against flesh, and a voice cried out.

The doors were hung with cardboard silhouettes of sea creatures for easy identification. The fourth on the left had a starfish. Stephen paused a moment, took a breath. Then he opened the door and stepped inside. He quickly closed it behind him and checked the corners on either side. But no one was there. The only person in the room was seated on the bunk that lay perpendicular to his line of sight, beneath a porthole.

Melissa sprang from the bed and threw her arms around him.

"I'm so glad to see you!" She murmured into his neck. "When I heard...You don't know how scared I was. I thought they'd killed you!"

Then her lips were on his like fire, and she was pulling him back toward the bunk. They fell together, clutching and tearing at each other's clothing. Stephen let himself be carried away by excitement and emotion. All the feeling that had been welling up in him finally found a sink. He poured it out for her, and she took all of it. They moved together like two boxers, fast and desperate. For a time, they shut out everything around them, and the world was simple and pure.

It was dark when she fell against his chest and lay still, breathing slow and steady against him. The sun had set, and the only light was the odd sweep of a boat's light over the porthole. The sounds from the other cabins and the bar merged into a distant drone.

"Until I got your letter," she said at last. "Until then, I didn't know if I was alive or dead. If he'd killed you..."

"I'm all right," he said.

"Yes, I noticed that. More than all right." She laughed for a moment, but then her voice was serious once more. "You don't know how dangerous he is. He's killed people in Harmony Beach before when they got in his way. And if half the stories from up north are true..."

She sat up and turned on a dim light that cast long shadows through the cabin. "I hate him!" she said suddenly. "I just want him to go away, but he never will. He's got his hooks in Harmony Beach now. And in me. He's never going to let us go."

"Don't worry about him," said Stephen. "He's just a man. He bleeds like anybody else."

She turned to him, and he saw the fear in her eyes. "What are you saying?"

"He started this thing," Stephen said. "I'm going to finish it. I'm saying I'm going to kill him."

She took him in her arms and squeezed him close to her. She shook her head. "Oh lover, don't say that. Don't even think that. You don't know him. He's not someone you go up against. You'll never even get to him. Half the time he's up north taking care of business. When he's here...there's no getting close to him. He's got Stoski and his own little army. I couldn't stand losing you like that."

"I'm not going to challenge him to draw at high noon. There's always a way. I'll figure it out."

"I wish you wouldn't talk like that," she repeated. "Someone tried once. Some mob soldier from up north. I guess they figured he'd be easier down here, away from his base." She paused and shuddered. "I heard him screaming from the other end of the house. Then they took something out to a boat and headed out. They came back a little later without it. Just don't talk that way, please."

Stephen gathered her in and held her.

"There's a better way to hurt him," she said quietly after a long moment.

Stephen moved her back to see her face. "What?"

"He's trying to expand his operations back home," she said. "It's all he talks about. So all that money he's squeezing out of Harmony Beach is going north. It's all in cash so the Feds can't trace it. He packs it all in a trunk and takes it up with him. But there's always tons of it there in the house. If we took it, that would hit him where it hurts. And we could disappear into the islands and find someplace where we can be together and never come back here again."

Stephen thought about it for a moment. "You know where he keeps it?"

She nodded. "We could do it when Ellis goes up north. He'll take a lot of cash with him, but there's always plenty left over. And he takes some of the guys with him and leaves Stoski in charge. It will be easier then."

"I'm sure he doesn't just leave it lying around," said Stephen. "It'll be locked up and guarded, right?"

"I know my way around the house," she said. "I know where he keeps the keys. And they're still building. You go down a hall and suddenly you're outside. There's stairways that go nowhere. He wants an indoor pool, but you can't dig down because you'll just hit water, so they're pouring cement to build it up above ground. It's a huge mess of a place. There's all kinds of places to hide, and ways into parts of the house where they won't see us. I can get us in."

Stephen looked at her. She looked hungry. She looked like she wanted him. She thought this would work. He could see it in her eyes and the set of her jaw. Of course he'd need to know a lot more about Kusack's resources and his routines than he knew right now. He'd need to know how many men guarded the house and how they operated. He'd need the layout of the place, schedules, copies of keys. It would take time, and he'd have to watch the place himself. That would mean going to Harmony Beach and hiding out there, avoiding Kusack's men and the Sheriff's goons.

Melissa's house would do as a base of operations. From what she'd told him, Kusack never went there. He was either at his own house or the club. So her place would let him hide out during the day. Then he could slip out at night and watch the mansion from the darkness.

The more he thought about it, the more he thought it could work. And it would feel good to kick Kusack in the balls first. Especially if it got them enough money to get away and set themselves up someplace in the islands. There would still be time to put a bullet into Kusack's shriveled heart later.

"Can you draw it for me?" he asked finally.

She smiled, then she took his hand and pulled him to her. "Anything you need, baby."

∼

COLIN TOOK what little was his and closed up the house himself. Stephen could open it up again if he ever came back. He gathered the farm workers and told them the rumrunning operation was finished. He had enough cash on hand to pay them what they were owed, with enough left over to get him staked if he was careful. He found himself wondering if he'd ever be back here himself. Now it occurred to him that he would miss Beckers Cay, though heaven knew he'd never missed it before. Time and the world were still changing him. What was he becoming now, he wondered.

"You be careful," Marcus told him as he was leaving. "Watch out for yourself, all alone out there."

"I'll be fine," Colin reassured him. "What about you? What are you going to do?"

"What I always do," said Marcus. "Fish and plant, and let it be enough." There was a hint of reproach in his tone.

"Well then you're a lucky man, Marcus. I hope I can come back and see how you're doing one day."

"You do that," said Marcus.

Then Colin loaded his few possessions aboard *Pegasus*, climbed aboard, and fired up the engine. Marcus cast off his mooring line, and with a last wave, Colin turned and headed out to sea.

He made for Nassau. He could get the bullet damage to *Pegasus'* woodwork repaired there. If he was lucky, the replacement parts he'd ordered for the Lion engine might be waiting. And there was always the casino at the Bahamian Club. He'd scraped out a living there before. He could do it again if nothing else presented itself.

He pulled into Nassau Harbor before sunset and wandered the waterfront neighborhoods, getting himself reacquainted with the town. His old place was still available, a couple rooms over a tobacco shop where he could smell the gentle odors of Black Cavendish and Cuban cigars. He was settled in again by dinner time, and it was as if he'd never left. He had dinner at his favorite restaurant and called it an early night.

As he lay in bed, the sounds of the nightlife rising up from the dark streets to his open window, he wondered about his brother. Where had Stephen gone? What was he doing? Was he safe? Stephen had made it very clear that he wasn't prepared to accept any advice. Colin had been let off the hook as surely as anyone could be. He was not his brother's keeper, at his brother's insistence.

But that still didn't satisfy him. As he fell toward sleep, the thought that he'd let the family down, that he'd disappointed his mother, crossed his mind and wouldn't leave him in peace.

The next few days were quiet and commonplace. Colin found a boatwright with a supply of good teak to repair the damage to *Pegasus*. The boatwright raised an eyebrow at the bullet scars, but he didn't ask questions. He assured Colin that he could do the work. He promised that no one would ever know the wood had been replaced.

Then Colin visited his favorite tailor and ordered a new tuxedo. He began watching the Bahamian Club from a cafe across the street, seeing who spent their time there these days. He found himself slipping readily back into his old routines. But his nights were still troubled by his worries about Stephen. He didn't even know how to contact him. He wrote Marcus on Beckers Cay with his address and instructions to notify him if Stephen appeared there or made contact somehow. Then, unsure what else to do, he put on his new tuxedo and headed for the casino.

"Hey! Rumrunner!"

Colin turned at Joe's voice. He was outside the Bahamian Club, just about to head in. Joe was sitting on the edge of the fountain with her pants rolled up and her feet in the water. Her shoes sat on the marble beside her. She beckoned him over, and Colin realized she was a bit drunk.

"What are you doing here?" she asked as he sat beside her, facing away from the water. "Thought you and your brother were running booze to the thirsty masses of Florida."

Colin smiled and told her what had happened, from their initial success to the clash with Ellis Kusack and the battle at sea with *Fianna*.

"Bloody hell," she said. "So where's your brother, then?"

"I don't know," Colin admitted. "We had an argument, and he took off. Didn't want to give it up."

"Found he had a taste for danger, did he?"

"That and a woman."

"Oh!" Joe hooted. "You didn't tell me that part."

"Turns out she's Kusack's woman, but no matter. Stephen's gone head over heels for her. He's off the rails. I don't know what he's up to now."

Joe nodded. "Women. Tell me about it. Nice to have around, but you can lose your head if you're not careful."

They sat quietly for a few minutes, watching guests come and go.

"So why are you here again?" she asked eventually.

"What do you mean?"

"I mean I'm a little drunk, so maybe I'm just spinning my wheels here, but you seem about as lost as him right now. Why are you sitting here?"

Colin shrugged. "I don't know what else to do with myself. The rumrunning business seems to have run its course. I didn't have much of a future worked out even before that."

Joe sighed, pulled her dripping feet up from the fountain and spun around beside him.

"I like you, Ridley," she said. "You're fun to have around. You got balls. I said that, right? When you saved Roger?"

"You did. How is Roger, by the way?"

"Oh, fine. On the mend. Back in Cornwall. I've been thinking about what to do myself. I thought I might buy myself one of these islands. God knows they've got enough of them. Thought I might buy one and build my own resort out here. You'd make a fine manager. What do you think of that?"

Colin didn't know how seriously he should take Joe, especially when she was drunk. But it was an intriguing idea at that.

"I...I'm flattered, I guess."

"Well, I'll let you know if anything comes of it. But right now, it sounds like you need to go make sure your brother's okay. You'll feel like a damn fool if he goes and gets his head blown off, don't you think?"

Colin realized she was right. It didn't matter if Stephen wanted his help or not. Stephen was his little brother, and that was all that mattered. If nothing else, he'd made a promise to their mother.

"You're right," he said. He got up and headed out toward the street.

"Look me up when you get back," Joe called after him.

Colin was already busy putting together a list of what he'd need to buy with the rest of his money.

17

STEPHEN'S DAYS HAD BECOME DULL, ALMOST UNBEARABLY monotonous. He didn't dare leave Melissa's house in Harmony Beach for fear someone would spot him. Stoski's goons could be anywhere. Sheriff Mayhew and his thuggish deputies were patrolling. All it would take was a neighbor to wonder who he was.

So Stephen spent the days indoors. He stayed away from the windows and kept the curtains drawn. He kept quiet. Once there was knock at the door in the early afternoon and Stephen froze in mid-step in the small living room, not even breathing. The knock came once more, then a shadow fell across the drawn curtains on the front window. Finally they decided nobody was home and left. It was nearly a minute of shallow breaths—his heartbeat pounding in his chest—before Stephen moved again.

Melissa came when she could get away from Kusack and the club. But he never knew when that would be, and it was always too short a time before she had to leave again. Then Stephen would be alone in the quiet, stuffy house with his relentless thoughts. He imagined it was something like being in prison.

But the nights. Those belonged to him. He was like Dracula,

he joked to himself. When darkness fell over Harmony Beach, Stephen slipped out into the night and stalked the island. He came to know every path, every stand of trees, every rise and inlet along the beach. He learned to dodge the Sheriff's patrols and to avoid Kusack's security guards. He found a wooded spot well away from the road with a good view of Kusack's mansion.

He came to know the mansion very well indeed.

The mansion's center sat at the end of a long, looping driveway. An east-facing wing stretched off to one side with what he assumed was a guest house connected at the far end. That part of the house was finished and inhabited. But the other side of the house was a skeletal maze of wood, stone, metal, and cement.

The construction crews were always gone by the time he arrived, but Stephen could track what they'd accomplished in daylight, while he hid in Melissa's house. The wooden forms for pouring the cement pool were nearly finished now. They stood like a wooden moat on a stone plaza overlooking the sea. Scaffolding was going up along the foundations of what would become another wing. He could make out half a dozen ways to slip into the house without being seen.

Melissa had drawn a detailed floor plan. There were parts of the house she hadn't seen directly, but not many. It was easy enough to work out what had to be where. On the first floor of the east wing was a small, windowless room. It was at the back of the house, tucked between the main hall and the kitchen and pantry areas. The only way to reach it was through an otherwise useless corridor that wrapped around the pantry.

It had to be the counting room.

Stephen looked at the little square in awe. All the money went there, different streams of it converging in great piles of bills. There it would be counted and logged, the bills separated and bundled by type. Melissa had never been inside, but she'd seen people coming and going. Stoski's men would carry satchels in and out with the care one only used with the boss's money. A pair of accountants showed up periodically and would disappear into that room for hours. When they emerged, they would meet with Kusack in his office on the second floor of the east wing. Melissa was there sometimes to look pretty and to overhear. The numbers she overheard were stunning, well into the millions.

So Stephen watched. He studied the routines of the house, and he planned and waited for the chance to make his move.

It was a Thursday night when an unfamiliar motorboat appeared on the beach. The breeze off the water ruffled the branches above Stephen's blind. He'd piled sand and arranged palm fronds to hide himself from the house. He lay in the sand with a bottle of water and a pair of binoculars he'd found in Melissa's house. He'd been surprised at how well the binoculars worked at night. For some reason he'd thought they'd be useless in the dark, but he could see small lights from farther away, and could make out poorly lit shapes much more clearly. And of course he could see more detail around the lit areas of the house.

He was scanning the north wing, studying the day's construction, when he heard the boat. The motor was a small outboard, a sound Stephen recognized immediately. It was odd that one would be out at night. He turned and swept the waves until he spotted it. It was coming down the beach from the north, from the club most likely. One man sat in the back and steered. He cut the engine and beached the boat, then got out and waited beside it as the waves lapped at the hull.

That was odd. The house had a dock and a covered boathouse located around the tip of the island's southern point. Perhaps someone might bring something down from the club by boat if there wasn't a car handy. But then why beach the boat here? And what was he waiting for?

Then a sound near the house caught Stephen's attention. He turned and saw a small group of men emerge from a back door. They threaded their way through the construction and headed down to the beach. Stephen counted six of them. Four were Stoski's men in their suits. No, he realized, the one in back was Stoski himself!

Stephen didn't recognize the other two men they were hustling down to the beach. They were dressed differently, in dark pants and shirts. Stoski's men gripped them by both arms, and they struggled and pleaded as they passed the forms for the swimming pool. Stephen couldn't make out words, but the tone was clear enough. The two men were terrified. Stephen felt a cold tendril of fear wrap around his own heart. He had a terrible intuition of what he was about to see.

When they reached the beach, they forced the two men to their knees. Stoski backhanded one of them and, through the binoculars, Stephen saw the shape of a pistol in his hand. The man he hit fell on his side in the sand, and Stoski's men hauled him back up.

Then Stoski walked around them, gesturing and talking. Again, Stephen couldn't make out the words, but the tone of voice was clear enough.

Suddenly, Stoski leveled his pistol and shot one of the men in the back of the head. That Stephen heard clearly enough. There was a bang, a flash of light from the muzzle, and the man just toppled forward like a felled tree and landed face down in the sand.

The other one screamed, and Stoski shot him as well. He fell forward beside his companion. Stoski stood over them, his gun arm still extended.

Stephen dropped the binoculars in the sand. *Jesus.* That was murder! He'd just seen two men murdered in cold blood. His heart was pounding, and he could feel himself beginning to sweat. It was all he could do to stay still in his blind.

Despite himself, he picked up the binoculars and watched as Stoski's men tossed the corpses into the boat. The man who'd brought the boat and one other climbed in after them, and the others pushed the boat back out into the surf. The pilot yanked the starter cord until the engine sputtered to life.

On the beach, one of the men produced a small folding spade, an army entrenching tool. He dug in the sand where the bodies had fallen, turning it over. Blood, Stephen realized. He was hiding the blood.

Stoski was already walking back up toward the house. The man with the spade finished his work, and the others followed him. The boat had already vanished into the night, heading out to sea. The beach was left empty, the incoming tide rolling gently up the sand. The waves left white streaks of foam as they receded and then rolled in again, and again, and again.

There was no indication at all that two men had just died here in fear and violence. It was as if nothing had happened.

Stephen lay there in the sand for more than an hour, waiting for things to calm down, for his own fear to subside. He started at every sound, convinced Stoski's men had discovered his hiding place and had come to flush him out. Alongside the fear, he felt shame. He felt weak and powerless, trapped there in a hole in the sand, afraid to move. Was this what Colin had felt, he wondered, crouching in a muddy trench under enemy fire? He thought about what it would be like to feel this way for months at a time. What if this were unending, punctuated only by occasional bursts of action and random deaths of the men on either side of you? Perhaps this was what had changed Colin so dramatically.

Finally, when the house was almost entirely dark, and the only sound was the rolling surf, Stephen forced himself to crawl back from his perch. He got to his feet with another small twinge of fear and made his way north toward Melissa's house.

He was still terrified. But he considered that fear as he walked through the night toward the village. It would take courage to kill Ellis Kusack, but he'd been filled with terror. Was he finished? Did he mean to back away from his plan?

No, he realized. He still hated Kusack, like a smoldering coal in his heart. It hadn't gone out. He was afraid, but courage was different from fearlessness. He was as determined as ever. There was something reassuring in that.

He slipped between the dark houses at the edge of the village and over the faded wooden fence into Melissa's back yard. As he opened the back door into the kitchen, he heard her gasp. Melissa came running from the living room. As Stephen closed the door, she threw herself at him and clutched him to her body. He could see that she'd been crying.

"Oh thank God! You're all right! When I heard…"

"What did you hear?"

"It was all over the club," she said, the words pouring out of her in a rush. "They caught someone trying to rob Ellis's house. I was sure it was you!"

She held him at arm's length for a moment, as if to reassure herself he was unhurt. Then she led him by the hand back into the living room. "I've been going crazy. I had to leave the club. I couldn't take it. What they would have done to you…I couldn't bear to even think about it."

"I know what they did," Stephen said quietly. "I saw it."

Her eyes widened. "Did they…"

Stephen nodded. "Stoski shot them. They put them on their knees on the beach, and Stoski flat out executed them. Then they threw the bodies in a boat and dumped them at sea."

"Oh, God." She had a half-empty bottle on a table by the sofa. She poured herself another drink and one for Stephen.

"There were two of them," Stephen said. "Any idea who they could have been?"

Melissa shook her head. "From the mainland most likely. We'd have heard if they were from here. Some of those rednecks up around Okeechobee might be crazy enough to try it."

She turned to him with sudden intensity.

"Stephen, I changed my mind. I don't want to do this anymore. We have to call it off."

He'd been expecting that. He could see how spooked she was. But he'd settled it in his mind. Danger or not, fear or not, Ellis Kusack owed him, and he was going to collect.

"No," he said calmly. "We can still do it."

She reacted with shock and nearly spilled her drink. "But this changes everything! You saw it. What they did! Maybe if it hadn't happened, that'd be one thing, but they'll be on alert now! It'll be three times as hard to get in. And Ellis is coming back any day. Once he gets here, it'll be too late. We should just call it off and get out of here."

He gave her a smile that he hoped showed confidence. "Hey," he said, "it's all right. What's this? I thought you were supposed to be tough?" He grinned and hugged her. He could feel her trembling against his chest.

"I am," she said. "You have to be tough around here. But this is too much. Every day wondering if you're going to get caught sneaking around. If someone's going to see you here. If Mayhew and his deputies are going to find you. Now this. It's too much."

She extricated herself from his arms and looked him in the eye. "Are you doing this because you think you have to prove something to me? Because you don't! I'm not a prize you get if you beat Ellis. I can make my own choices, and I chose you."

"I know," he said. "It's not like that. This isn't about you." Then he grinned again. "Well, the money's for us. But my beef with Kusack's about me and him. I've got to settle it."

He sat down on the sofa and beckoned her to join him.

"This doesn't change anything," he said as she sat beside him. "They'll think they got rid of the threat. Everybody's in a panic up at the club, aren't they? Word will get around, and nobody will dare come within a mile of the place. That's the perfect time to hit them."

Melissa looked uncertain, but Stephen pressed on. "But I do think you should get out of town."

"No! How are you going to do it without me? I know the place. I know—"

"You told me all I need," said Stephen. "I could walk around that house blindfolded by now. But it is going to be dangerous. I'll be better off if I know you're safe. Can you get a ride out to the Rum Line?"

"I guess I can, yeah."

"Leave your boat in that mangrove stand on the bay side of the property. They won't find it there." He smiled. "They don't want to get their suit pants wet."

"I can do that."

"I'll get it done, and I'll meet you out there."

"I don't know, Stephen. What if you don't show? What am I going to do?"

"I'll be there," he said, making his voice as reassuring as he could. "I know what I'm doing." He forced down the cold fingers of doubt that drummed in the back of his mind. The world he'd known on the farm was over. It was time to move out into the larger world, and that world would test him. It was time to prove that he had what it took to step out of the neat pigeonhole life had given him and choose his own path. The war had been Colin's test. Ellis Kusack was his.

Stephen didn't mean to fail that test.

1 8

PEGASUS DROVE STEADILY WEST TOWARD THE RUM LINE. AHEAD OF her was the setting sun, behind her an ominous line of dark clouds. A squall was moving in behind him. In the cockpit, Colin avoided his worry for Stephen by listening closely to the Lion engine, roaring away beneath its fairing. The new parts had been installed, checked, and tuned. The sound was slightly different than before, but only Colin knew the engine well enough to notice that. It was running to spec, slightly above in fact, and was good as new. The repaired woodwork had been polished to a bright gleam. His boat was fully recovered and ready for action.

The only question was what to do? He had no idea what his brother was planning, but he assumed he would have passed through the Rum Line. If luck was with him, Stephen might still be there. More likely, he'd headed on to Harmony Beach. That would be his next stop once he'd learned what he could aboard the freighters.

They appeared ahead of him, at first a clutch of smoke tendrils rising from stacks. Then he saw the lights and the dark outlines of the ships. Something was different, he saw as he powered into the clutch of smaller boats. The Rum Line was a flurry of activity. The freighters were scattering, pulling up their boarding platforms and steaming out. On the smaller boats, men were shouting and waving handfuls of cash for one last deal.

"You buying?" a leather-tanned man shouted from a loaded fishing boat as he passed. Colin cut the throttle.

"What's going on? Where's everybody going?"

The man pointed east at the darkened sky with an incredulous look. "Haven't you heard, buddy? There's a storm coming in! A hurricane! Headed right for us!"

Colin's heart fell. Of course. He hadn't had time to concern himself with the weather. But it was the season for storms. The line of angry clouds behind him could indeed be much more than a mere squall.

"You buying?" the man repeated. "It's last call. For a while anyhow."

Colin shouted thanks and cruised on. He scanned the ships. At least one still had the welcome sign out, the *Edmund Kitts*. He made for her, tied *Pegasus* at the edge of the platform, and headed up to the deck.

They wouldn't be here long, he saw as he reached the top of the stairs. An officer shouted orders at a group of sailors taking down the lights and brightly colored banners from the superstructure. He stopped one of them.

"I'm looking for my brother," he said. "Name's Stephen Ridley. He would have been through maybe a week ago." He started to describe him, but the sailor looked at him as if he were crazy.

"Sorry, pal," he said, and he hurried off.

In the hold, the situation wasn't much different. Shouts echoed off the bulkheads until they became an almost painful wall of noise. A man who Colin assumed was the Captain stood in front of the bar, mobbed by runners waving money. He was auctioning off the last of his cargo at whatever price it would bring.

A dour-faced sailor stood to one side with a pistol in his belt and a dark, polished billy club in his hands, ready to maintain order by force if necessary. Colin tried to ask him about Stephen, but again got nowhere.

"Colin! Colin Ridley!"

He turned at the voice to see Melissa hurrying across the hold. She looked frantic. He looked around for some sign of Kusack or his thugs, but she was alone.

"I'm so glad to see you!" she said as she reached him. "They're getting ready to go. Everyone's pulling out, and I don't know what to do!"

"Where's Stephen?" Colin asked urgently. "Have you seen him?"

"He's back at Harmony Beach," she said. "We were going to rob Ellis's house. But everything's gone wrong!"

"Come here," he said, taking her arm and pulling her toward a hatch to the aft cabins. He could hardly hear her with all the noise.

It was quieter when they reached the rows of cabins, though not by much. A woman in garish makeup and a beaded flapper dress hurried past them with a suitcase in one hand and panic in her eyes. In a cabin, someone was singing "Keep the home fires burning, til the boys come home!" Whoever he was, he was very drunk. Chaos seemed to be overtaking the Rum Line ahead of the approaching storm, and what little order there had been was quickly breaking down.

Colin found a stairway and led Melissa down into a machinery space. The place smelled of burnt oil, but at least it was quieter.

"Now start at the beginning," he told her. "What's Stephen doing?"

She told him how Stephen had hidden in her house and cased Kusack's mansion by night, planning to slip in and steal the cash he kept there. But then someone else had gotten the same idea and been caught. She'd wanted to call it off then, she said, but Stephen refused.

"He sent me out here," she concluded. "He said he'd do the job himself."

Colin swore. "He's going to get himself killed," he said angrily. "What the hell makes him think he can pull that off?"

"Ellis is up north," Melissa said. "Joe Stoski's running the house, but a lot of the guys went with Ellis. And I know the house. I told him how to get in. It's not as bad as it sounds."

Colin doubted that, but he knew Stephen would go for it hook, line, and sinker. Between his hatred of Kusack and his newfound addiction to danger, keeping Stephen alive was starting to become a problem.

"So say this damn fool scheme actually goes like he thinks. What's he going to do? Is he coming here?"

"We hid my motorboat near the house," she said. "He was going to meet me here with the money. But there won't be anything here! There's nowhere for him to go. When this storm hits, he won't have any way out of Harmony Beach. He'll be trapped on the island."

Colin's mind raced. If the storm that followed him across from the islands really was a full-blown hurricane, then just riding it out on a barrier island would be dangerous enough. Trying to head out to sea in a small motorboat would be madness.

"What do we do?" Melissa asked.

"We go get him," said Colin. There was nothing else he could do. The first step was to get to Harmony Beach and find out what he was dealing with. If he was lucky, he'd be able to head Stephen off before he did anything too stupid. But that was asking a lot, he told himself. More likely, he'd need to get Stephen out of whatever mess he'd gotten into. Then they could worry about the storm.

The deck rolled beneath him as he considered what to do.

The wind was picking up, whipping up the surface. The storm was coming in fast behind them. It was time to go.

"Do you have to get anything?" he asked Melissa. She shook her head.

He led her up the stairs, back to the cabin deck. He was just clearing the top of the stairs when something slammed into his head from behind. He pitched forward and fell to the deck. He heard Melissa gasp behind him, then a figure charged around the stairway railing and kicked him hard in the jaw. Colin felt his head snap back and his vision went blurry. He lay stunned as his attacker quickly frisked him and took his wallet.

As his vision cleared, he saw a long, gleaming blade. The man thrust it threateningly toward Melissa.

"Piss off, Missy, or I'll gut you too."

He knew that voice. Scogins.

"Knew I'd run across you again," Scogins said, leaning over Colin with the knife pointed at his throat. "Small world out here."

Melissa had disappeared. Colin tried to sit up, but Scogins slashed the air in front of him with the knife, and Colin pulled back.

"What do you want, Scogins? Your beef's not with me." As he played for time, his eyes swept the deck looking for something he could use as a weapon, but he saw nothing.

"Oh yeah, it is," said Scogins with a leer. Colin could smell the whiskey on his breath. "You did me wrong, pretty boy. You're going to pay."

"Jesus, you sound like my brother. I should show you to him. You can be an example of why he shouldn't think that way."

"You're funny," said Scogins. "I'll give you another grin you can laugh out of."

Then he sprang, leading with the knife. Colin swept his arm up to block Scogins's wrist, and the blade missed his throat by inches. It struck the deck, and then the two of them were rolling on the deck, grappling for the blade. They slammed into the bulkhead and Scogins grunted in pain. Colin sank a punch into his midsection, but Scogins just shook it off and kicked Colin off him.

The knife lay on the deck between them, but Scogins got to it first and rolled to a crouch as Colin got up. He made a wild, defensive slash in the air between them, and Colin fell back. The boat rolled, and his shoulders hit the bulkhead behind him just as Scogins sprang. Colin caught his knife arm, and they strained against each other. Scogins tried to force the blade into Colin's face, and Colin could only push back with what leverage he could muster with his body forced awkwardly against the bulkhead.

The point slipped closer to his eyes. Colin stamped Scogins' foot and instep, but Scogins wore heavy leather boots with reinforced toes. It didn't phase him at all. Colin was fighting to turn to the side and let the thrust go into the bulkhead beside him. But then a figure appeared behind Scogins. Colin heard glass shattering, and then his face was sprayed with rum.

Scogins went limp and collapsed into a heap on the deck. Behind him stood Melissa with the dripping remains of a broken bottle.

"You okay?" she asked.

Colin nodded as he caught his breath. Scogins was out cold, soaked in rum, and bleeding from his scalp. Colin tossed the knife down the stairs into the machinery room. He checked Scogins' pockets and retrieved his wallet.

Melissa studied Scogins' face. "Who the hell is this guy, and what's he got against you?"

Colin shook his head. "Doesn't matter. He's nothing to worry about."

"Yeah, now he's not," said Melissa with a grin. She dropped the bottle neck on the deck.

"Thank you," said Colin, and the boat rolled beneath them once again. "It's getting worse. We need to go."

They made their way back to the hold, where the auction had

apparently ended. The hold was nearly empty, and the crew had disappeared to other parts of the ship. On deck, they found them battening down hatches and preparing to get underway.

"If you don't want to go to Cuba with us, you'd best get going!" one shouted as they headed for the stairs.

"Just leaving!" Melissa called back.

A crew was already gathering at the top of the stairs. Colin and Melissa hurried down, and he got her aboard *Pegasus*. As they cast off, the crew was hauling in the floating platform and bringing up the stairs. Colin fired up the engine and backed away from the freighter. Most of the small boats had already gone, and the *Edmund Kitts* was the last of the big freighters still in place. The floating wild west town on the Rum Line had vanished as suddenly as it had appeared.

Colin steered around to the west. The waves were rough now, and the wind whipped through his hair as he pointed the bow toward Harmony Beach. The sky behind them was black and threatening. He had no trouble believing it was a hurricane coming in to scour its way across Florida. The quicker he found Stephen, the better.

Colin opened up the throttle and *Pegasus* smashed through the choppy water. They raced toward Harmony Beach as the storm dogged their heels.

STEPHEN CROUCHED IN HIS BLIND IN THE RAIN, WATCHING THE house below. The rain and the overcast made it hard to see what was going on even with the binoculars. That was good, he told himself. He might be cold and soaking wet now, but once he got moving, that would be forgotten. Around him the tree branches swayed in the rising wind. The rain would muffle his footsteps, make him harder to spot, and encourage Kusack's men to huddle inside.

A good-sized storm could only help him, he thought. As long as it didn't get *too* big.

This was hurricane season after all, and the eastern sky looked ominous. He could see whitecaps whipping up as the waves rolled into the beach. Once he got out of the house, he'd need to take Melissa's small boat out into that, and that didn't appeal to him.

One step at a time. Get the money first. Perhaps it was just a passing squall.

Stephen wore jeans and a dark cotton shirt. Instead of his usual boots, he wore a pair of rubber-soled tennis shoes so he could move quickly and quietly. Over his shoulder was an army haversack of olive drab canvas. Inside it was a pistol he hoped he wouldn't need, along with a crowbar and two tightly folded duffel bags for the money. The haversack and duffel bags were waxed to keep out water. Stephen grinned. He might get soaked to the bone out here, but the money would be safe and dry.

He had his course planned out and memorized. He'd move quickly down the slope to the partially constructed north wing where the scaffolding and forms would conceal his approach. There was a doorway there, covered to keep out the weather until more construction enclosed it. That was how he would enter the house. There was a service corridor that would take him behind the main entry hall, the dining rooms, and other spaces whose purpose wasn't really clear to him. It would lead past the kitchens, perhaps the most dangerous part of the trip. But past there was a door that would let him into the plain, windowless corridor that led to the counting room. He would fill the duffel bags and make his way out the same way he'd come.

He was as ready as he was going to be. He took a deep breath and was just about to break cover and head down the slope when light poured out of the front doors. Stephen froze and watched. A half dozen men emerged, led by Joe Stoski. They wore suits and long, dark rain jackets. He noticed that two of them carried rolled up umbrellas. The rain soaked them as they stood with umbrellas and didn't unfurl them. A pair of cars emerged from the long garage on the far side of the drive, headlights lancing through the rain. The men piled in, and the cars headed off down the drive toward the road.

Kusack, Stephen realized. Melissa had said he was coming back soon. He must be arriving tonight, and Stoski was taking a detail to retrieve him from the train station on the mainland.

It was a sign, he told himself. There would never be a better time than now. The house must be practically deserted. He watched the taillights disappear down the long, palm-lined drive, and then glanced out to sea at the growing storm. Then he broke out of the blind and hurried down the slope, his feet sliding in the loose sand.

He made the cover of the construction area and pressed his back tight against a plywood form. He listened for some indication that he'd been seen, but all he heard was the drumming of rain on the wood. He looked around the edge and saw no movement, no new lights. His heart was pounding in his chest and suddenly he ripped off the haversack and dug through it for the pistol he'd bought on the Rum Line. It was a .45 caliber Colt automatic, heavy and threatening. He stuck it in his belt at his back where he'd be able to reach it if he needed it. Then he slung the pack over his shoulder again and took a deep breath.

He was alive with the thrill of danger. His senses seemed heightened far beyond their normal state. He could feel every raindrop impact his skin, sense the scaffolding giving way before the wind. He suddenly drew the pistol from behind his back and pointed at an imaginary target on the beach. His reflexes were tuned like Colin's precious racing engine. He was afraid, yes, but he also felt powerful, fast, and strong. He could do anything. This was what he'd felt when they'd run rum past the eyes of the Coast Guard, when they'd confronted Kusack, when he'd drawn his pistol on Scogins among a dozen armed men.

He'd missed this feeling. He needed it.

He made his way around the forms for the swimming pool in a fast moving crouch and entered the maze of masonry and lumber that was the north wing. Nothing interrupted him as he reached the doorway into the house. When all this was finished, the spot where Stephen stood would be an observation gallery, Melissa had told him. The landward side of the hall would be lined with doors for guests' rooms and a lounge. On the other side would be a long row of windows looking out across the beach to the sea. The portal in front of him would have a light interior door leading into the main part of the house. But right now there was only cement foundations and framing. The doorway was covered over with a sheet of hardwood plywood nailed into a frame of two-inch studs.

Stephen took the crowbar from his pack and jammed the blade into the seam between the plywood and its frame. This part would make some noise; that couldn't be helped. But again the storm was helping him. He could hear the wind howling around the corners of the house, and the rattling and groaning of the scaffolds. If anyone heard him ripping the door open, he hoped they'd think it was just more of the same.

He leaned into the crowbar and felt the nails pulling loose with a grating sound. He knelt down to pull out the bottom edge, again with a shriek and pop as the nails came free. For a moment he turned his back to the wall and crouched there with the crowbar raised in one hand and his other hand ready to go for the gun. But nobody came. No one had heard him.

He set the crowbar down beside the doorway and pulled hard on the bottom of the plywood. It was heavy wood, hard to bend, and for a moment he thought he might have to take it off entirely. But he managed to make a gap big enough to slip through. Then he let it go back. There was still a gap where he'd separated it, and the plywood vibrated in the wind. Rain began seeping in through the gap and pooling on the floor. Stephen left wet tracks and bits of sand behind as he headed down the hall.

Someone would notice that if they passed this way. Speed was called for now. In and out as quickly as he could manage. He heard the house creaking in the rising wind, but he heard no voices or footsteps.

He hurried down the service corridor, past the double doors to the dining room. He could see the kitchen ahead, a faint light spilling out. He moved against the wall and edged up to the doorway, listening. He heard a ticking sound, like a spoon clicking against china. A few moments later it came again, a faint click. He visualized someone in the kitchen with a cup of tea, someone who would see him and raise the alarm. He listened intently for some other sound, a voice, the scrape of a chair against the floor. But there was only silence. Then the same sound again. *Tap.*

Stephen began to wonder if there was a person there at all. Whether there was or wasn't, he couldn't just sit crouching at the edge of the kitchen door until someone came along. He drew the pistol from his belt and took one deep breath, then another. Then Stephen sprang around the doorframe and leveled the gun in front of him in both hands.

The kitchen was empty. Stephen frantically looked around, even up on top of the cabinets. But there was no one. Then the tapping sound came again, and this time he saw what caused it. A drop had fallen from the faucet into dishes stacked in the sink. *Tap.*

Stephen sighed and shook his head. He would leave this part out when recounting his heroics to Melissa later on.

He tightened the faucet valve until the drop stopped growing on the lip. Then he moved quietly back to the hallway.

The next door was the one he wanted. He held the gun in his right hand and leaned over to slowly open it with his left. It was dark in the hall, so dark he couldn't see the corner where the hallway turned to the left. There would be a light switch somewhere, but Stephen didn't feel for it. Who might notice if he turned the lights on?

Instead he slipped through and closed the door behind him. He stood for a moment in the deep darkness and listened. He heard nothing, so he put his left hand on the wall and felt his way gingerly forward. He slid his feet slowly forward lest he kick something and make a noise. It seemed to take forever to reach the corner.

Around the corner, the hallway continued another twenty feet to a narrow strip of light from beneath a door. That would be the counting room, where the money was waiting for him. He edged down the hallway, a little quicker now, drawn by the sheer gravity of the money on the other side of that door.

Then he stopped. A shadow moved across the bar of light. Someone was inside. Stephen let out a breath he hadn't realized he'd been holding. Of course someone was there. If he had that much cash lying around, he'd have someone guarding it.

Stephen drew the Colt, squeezed the grips and felt its reassuring weight in his hand. This was it. He was on unfamiliar ground now, walking into a room with a gun to threaten someone's life. It wasn't the kind of man he wanted to be. But these were special circumstances, he told himself. Ellis Kusack's money. Kusack's soldiers.

God, what if there was more than one? What would he do if there were half a dozen armed men in there?

He edged up to the door and listened intently. All he heard was the wind wailing around the house.

The storm was rising. He couldn't sit here all night. If he was going to do this, he had to move quickly and get out before the seas got too rough. It wouldn't do to get trapped on the barrier island, caught between a storm and Kusack's army of killers.

He was about to reach for the knob when the door suddenly opened. The light from inside spilled out, and a hand reached out, feeling on the wall for the light switch.

Stephen's fears and doubts vanished like smoke, and he acted on instinct. He grabbed the arm by the wrist and hauled the owner off balance. He stumbled out into the hallway, and Stephen jammed the pistol's muzzle under his chin. The man gave a startled *gawp*.

"Sshh. Quiet. If you make even a little sound, I'll make a real big one. You got it?"

The man nodded furiously. He didn't look like a mob torpedo. He was in his late forties, thinning hair, glasses. He looked more like an accountant.

"Back inside," Stephen ordered him, and they moved through the door together like a pair of ballroom dancers. Stephen closed the door behind him.

Money was everywhere.

It lay in stacks all over the large table in the center of the room. Some were short, some were tall. More money sat in banded stacks on shelves along the walls. The shelves were labeled with denominations. Twenties here, hundreds there. The room was a library of cash.

Stephen felt himself gawking and pulled back to the man at the end of his gun.

"Who are you?"

"Nobody!" he stammered. "I'm Willis. I'm just a clerk! I don't have a gun or anything!"

Stephen gestured toward one end of the table. There was a chair, an ashtray with a still-smoldering butt, a pile of paper bands. "You count the money, Willis? Band it up, get it ready to go?"

Willis nodded. "That's right."

"How much is in here, then?"

Willis swallowed. "Right now...a little more than three and a half million dollars."

Stephen let out a low whistle. "Who says crime doesn't pay? All right, Willis. Do as you're told, and you won't get hurt."

He shrugged off the haversack and knelt down to remove the two duffel bags. He tossed them to Willis.

"Fill these up. Start with the hundreds over there. You know, I don't even think we can get all this into these two bags. But by God, we're going to try."

Willis got to work filling the bags, and Stephen studied the rest of the room. Beyond the table was an open area with a smaller, round wooden table and several cane back chairs. Unlike the immaculate counting table, this smaller one was scarred with gouges and cigarette burns. There was a mostly empty whiskey bottle on its side. Stephen imagined Kusack's men sitting here, perhaps playing cards while they watched the money being counted.

"Why are you down here all alone in the middle of the night, Willis?" he asked.

Willis was busily stuffing bills into one of the bags. "Well there was a…someone tried to rob the place before."

"Yeah, I know."

"With Mr. Kusack coming back tonight, Mr. Stoski wanted a recount. Just to be sure."

Stephen chuckled. "I don't think he's going to like the results, is he? All right, put that over by the door and get started on the other one."

Willis hurriedly filled the second bag while Stephen considered what to do with him. He couldn't let him go alert whoever else was still in the house. He should have thought of this, brought some handcuffs or something. He'd just have to make do with what he had.

When Willis had stuffed both bags nearly to bursting, Stephen waved him over to the round table. Willis nervously obeyed.

"Take off your shirt," Stephen ordered him.

"My shirt?"

"And your socks and shoes too."

He sat Willis in one of the cane back chairs, his arms behind him, and tied him to the chair with his own shirt. Then he stuffed his socks into his mouth.

"Can you breathe through your nose all right?"

Willis tried it and nodded.

"All right then. Someone will be along sooner or later. When Kusack asks you what happened, tell him it was Stephen Ridley that took his money. And his woman. Be sure and tell him that part too. You got it?"

Willis nodded and made a faint sound through his socks.

"Tell him."

Then Stephen hurried to the door and hefted the two duffel bags. They were surprisingly heavy. He wouldn't be moving gracefully, light on his feet. But that was just fine with him. He looked around at the shelves. As he suspected, he hadn't cleaned out the room entirely, but he'd made a major dent in Kusack's nest egg. He guessed there was more than a million dollars in each of the bags.

A particularly strong gust of wind shook the house, as if to remind him he was on the clock. The storm was still growing. If he wanted to get out of here, it was time to go.

Stephen opened the door a crack. It was dark and quiet in the hallway outside. He slung one of the heavy bags over his shoulder, carried the other in his left hand and his .45 in his right. Then he opened the door with his foot and headed back out into the dark.

STEPHEN KICKED THE PLYWOOD SHEET HARD. IT GAVE A LITTLE BUT remained in place, so he stepped back and then sprang forward, thrusting with one leg. This time there was a loud shriek, and it tore away from the frame. The wind caught it and flipped it against the scaffolding with a bang.

Stephen bent down to pick up the duffel bags. That was more noise than he'd hoped there would be, and the missing cover was more likely to draw attention. But it couldn't be helped. There was no way he was squeezing through the gap he'd left on the way in with the duffel bags in tow. He just needed to move fast, before someone could investigate.

The wind and rain whipped him as he stepped out into the night. The wind off the sea was strong enough now to knock over scaffolds and tear fronds off the palm trees. Stephen bent his head against the wind and hurried up the slope toward his old hiding place. This was a time for quickness, not for stealth.

He cleared the ridge and turned left, heading toward the stand of mangroves where Melissa's boat was waiting. If he was careful, he would be under cover of trees all the way there except for a quick dash across the driveway.

The trees swayed and murmured around him. He heard a branch crack behind him and fall crashing to the ground. This was a lousy night to be out. It was no kind of night to be at sea in a small boat either. He began to think it might be better to head for the mainland instead and shelter somewhere until the storm blew over.

As he approached the driveway, he stopped at the edge of the trees and set the bags down. They were heavy, and it was hard going with them over the loose, sandy ground. He crouched there to catch his breath and watch the house. The drive itself was dark. Nothing moved. He could see the lights of the house in the distance, but there was nothing to suggest an alarm had been raised. The rain soaked through his clothes, stung his bare skin, and dripped off him to pool around his feet. He gave himself another minute, but no more. He had a head start. Maybe he could get more of one. He needed all he could get.

Stephen hefted the two duffel bags, took a deep breath, and ran across the driveway. Even though he'd seen no one, he half feared the crack of a gunshot and a bullet tearing into his body. But he made it across and back into the trees on the far side. From here, he would be in a part of the estate that Kusack had left untouched. Uncleared woods ran gradually downhill toward the marshy southern tip of the island. He'd get wet sloshing through the shallow water out to the boat, but that seemed redundant now.

Then he stopped suddenly. There was a light ahead of him, gleaming from behind a tree and illuminating the slashing raindrops. Stephen dropped the bags and crouched between them, the pistol in his hand. Someone else was out here. The light didn't move. He crept toward it in a low crouch. All he heard was the storm and the creaking trees. He didn't hear anyone, but someone must have brought that light out here.

He rounded a tree into a small clearing and found himself no more than an arm's reach from another man. They were both low to the ground, Stephen crouching, the other man bent over to dig with an Army surplus entrenching tool like the one Stephen had seen them use on the beach. He turned as Stephen rounded the tree, and they found themselves staring into each other's eyes, both too startled to react.

The man had been digging a long, low hole in the sandy ground. On the far side was a Coleman lantern that cast the light. Beside it, a double-barreled shotgun leaned against a tree.

For a moment, they looked at each other. The other man's eyes flicked nervously to his shotgun, out of reach. He tensed and sprang with the shovel.

Stephen was raising his pistol when the shovel smashed into his wrist. The gun flew free, but as the wild swing carried the other man past him, Stephen slammed his body against the tree and thrust a knee into his groin. The man whirled back with a groan, but Stephen grabbed the shovel and was able to wrench it from his hands. Before the other man could launch a counterattack, Stephen swung the shovel hard into his temple and the man collapsed like a dropped sack of grain.

Stephen stood over him, panting. His pistol had landed nearby, and he retrieved it. The other man was out cold. What was he doing here? He was less than a hundred yards from where the boat was waiting. That couldn't be coincidence.

He headed down toward the boat, and soon saw what had happened. He swore under his breath. Two men were aboard Melissa's boat, pushing it out through the mangroves. Another waited on the shore. This one had a Thompson gun.

He didn't see how these men could know what had happened at the house. But somehow they'd found the boat. The area must be patrolled after all. So they'd found the boat and realized someone would be coming for it. If they recognized it as Melissa's, maybe they suspected that person would be him. Either way, they were taking the boat away, probably back to the boathouse at the mansion. They were waiting for him to come back. And the hole the other man had been digging, higher up where it wouldn't just fill with water…

That was to be his grave.

Stephen slipped silently back, disappearing into the trees. The boat was a lost cause now. He made his way back to the clearing. The man he'd fought was still out. Stephen rolled him into the shallow grave and left him there. He considered taking the shotgun, but it would be too cumbersome. He was already overloaded. He took out the shells and threw them into the night. The entrenching tool, he took.

The bags were where he'd left them. He hefted them again and headed back the way he'd come. The plan had fallen apart at the end. He'd have to improvise now. There were two ways off the island: by water, or over the bridge to the mainland. He'd have to get his hands on a boat or a car. The closest place to do that would be the mansion. Kusack's long garage was a quarter of the way around the long approach loop to the house. A hundred yards behind that was the boathouse. There would be a couple small boats there, and probably Melissa's boat by the time he got there. He envisioned the route around the edge of the carefully maintained lawn to the garage, then around that and down to the boathouse.

It wasn't going to work, he realized. Not with the money. The route was too long, too open and exposed. Even if no one had found Willis in the counting room yet, the men who'd taken Melissa's boat would have the place on alert. He might make it if he was fast and careful enough, if he could surprise anyone guarding the boats. But there was no way he'd make it while hauling the two heavy bags. He took another look at the entrenching tool. He was going to have to bury the money and come back for it.

He looked around for a likely spot, studied the layout of trees and rocks. It wasn't easy in the dark, but he needed to be sure he could find the place again. The last thing he needed was to add another legendary lost treasure to the dozens of them supposedly waiting to be found along the Florida coast.

The land was rising to his left, so he followed the slope up and found himself on a low promontory overlooking the channel. A rock jutted up from the ground beneath a gnarled bald cypress tree. It would do, he decided. He could recognize this place from the water, even in the storm. He dropped the bags, unfolded the entrenching tool, and began to dig as the wind and rain lashed at him.

"Just like a pirate," he told himself as he dug.

When he was done he took the shovel with him. It might make a quiet weapon if he needed one. It had certainly put its previous owner out quickly enough. His .45 would just bring more trouble on the run, so he left the gun in his belt. He ran as quickly as he could through the storm, back toward the mansion.

He reached the drive and ran along the strip of mowed grass at the edge of the trees. He would cut back into the trees as he neared the house and make his way to the far side of the garage. From there, he'd be in the open down the sloping lawn toward the boathouse, and he'd have to pass through a well-lit gate. Hopefully no one would be there, but he couldn't be sure. The house's routine had been disrupted.

Stephen was still visualizing his route when he realized lights were approaching from behind. He veered into the trees and watched the convoy roll past him toward the house. There were four large cars, their engines roaring and rain lashing the metal. Kusack was back. Stephen swore under his breath and hurried toward the turn where the drive met the loop. From there he could see the cars pull up in a line in front of the house. Kusack's men started climbing out, turning their backs into the wind and rain.

They were hurrying for the front door, but then two men came out and stopped them. One was the typical Kusack goon. The other was Willis.

Lights were going on all over the house, and even the garage. Stephen couldn't hear over the wind, but Kusack was shouting orders, and men were spreading out, drawing weapons. The storm was forgotten for now.

So much for the boathouse. He'd never make it now. As if to confirm his fears, a couple men came running from around the corner of the garage, guns drawn.

He crouched in the trees and for the first time felt like a trapped animal. If he could make it to the club, he could take a boat there. That was nearly three miles of mostly open land to cover with Kusack's men hunting him. But he couldn't see any other way. Stephen headed back the way he'd come and turned toward the main road. Then he headed off the road toward the mainland side and started to hike north, past staked out lots where Ellis Kusack would one day build getaway villas for well-off tourists. The club seemed a very long way away indeed.

Still, he almost made it. He guessed he was a little less than a mile from the club when he saw the headlights. He crouched down and waited for the car to pass. He was well off the road, and there was no reason they should see him. It was coming from the north anyway. Probably just a club patron heading home.

But then a spotlight beam swept across him and stopped. Stephen's heart raced. It was the Sheriff. It had to be. And some-how, they'd seen him. The car veered off the road and rattled toward him, pinning him with headlights and the searchlight. He turned and ran, but soon realized that was no good. The terrain here was solid enough for the car to outrun him. In desperation he dropped the shovel and drew his pistol. If he could put a couple rounds into the engine, maybe that would stop them, and he could slip away into the darkness.

He fired into the glare, then kept firing until the gun ran dry. But he didn't even know if he'd hit the car. Then a chatter of automatic fire tore through the storm, muzzle flashes from both sides of the car. Thompson guns. Sheriff Mayhew had his deputies with him. They'd piled out and could be anywhere now.

"That's enough, boy!" the Sheriff shouted over the storm. "You want to live, you'd best cut that nonsense out! Put it down now."

The gun was useless now anyway. Stephen tossed it away and put his hands in the air.

He'd failed. He'd bet everything, including his life, on this throw of the dice, and now he'd blown it. He knew the Sheriff wouldn't shoot him here. No, Ellis Kusack would want to see him, and Kusack would have something much worse in store for him.

Then there was a sudden movement in the corner of his eye, something hit him hard in the temple, and Stephen went down in the wet, clinging sand. It went dark, and Stephen slipped away. The last pieces of awareness were the howl of the angry wind and the rain beating his face.

PEGASUS RACED THE STORM TOWARD LANDFALL WITH THE WIND AT
her back and the heavy sea chasing her stern. At the wheel, Colin
felt like he was falling through a dark void. The night behind him
was pitch dark and the sea ahead wasn't much better. He couldn't
see the lights of the coast. He kept an eye on the compass to
maintain a bearing toward Harmony Beach.

"We should land at the club," Melissa said. "See if they know
anything there."

It made sense. They needed a plan once they reached
Harmony Beach. It wouldn't do to charge in blind. Colin nodded
but said nothing.

"You don't like me much, do you?" Melissa said after another
minute of silence.

"I've got nothing against you," Colin replied. "You're just
tangled up with trouble, and my brother's too stupid to keep out
of it. That's not your fault."

"You shouldn't say that about him. He's not stupid."

"Oh yeah? This plan's not exactly the mark of an undiscov-
ered genius, sweetheart. What do you see in him anyway? Why

didn't you brush him off and send him on his way? That part I might blame you for."

She bristled. "All right, I'll tell you why. Sure he's cute, and he's fun to be with. But that's a lot of guys. You want to know why Stephen? Because he's never let me down. Not once. He's always done just what he said he'd do. That's more than I can say for Ellis. Or anyone else I've known."

Colin took that in. Yes, he thought, Stephen was stubborn, but he had to admit it was the good kind of stubborn. Mostly.

"This too," Melissa said. "He'll come through this. He's tough, and he's smart, and he's got guts. He'll make it."

Colin wondered if she was trying to convince him or herself. Either way, he knew his brother was brave, but that didn't matter. Stephen wasn't going to make it out of this one without help.

"My turn now." Melissa shouted over the engine. "What happened to you? What scared you so bad? Stephen keeps talking about how you're the tough one that went off to fight, and you know how the world works while he's never been far from where he grew up. It's all you running booze in your boat, and you're the big man in charge. I don't see it."

"Okay, that's how you think. I get the point."

"From here, you look timid as a church mouse. You let Ellis shove you off without a peep. Hell, I put up more of a fight. So what happened to you? Why aren't you who your brother thinks you are?"

Colin saw lights ahead. They were approaching Harmony Beach. He steered toward the channel.

"I've seen it happen," she said. "Men came back, and they weren't the same. There's no shame in it."

"The war changed me all right," Colin said. "But it wasn't shell shock. I wasn't just regular infantry in the trenches over there. That's how it was at first, but not for long. They pulled me out for special training, and then they sent me off to fight behind the scenes. I know how things work all right. I know good people die, and the bad ones claw their way through. I know enough to stay away from trouble if I can."

"You don't want to talk about it? With him at least?"

"I'm not *allowed* to talk about it," Colin said. "And if I could, I wouldn't. Especially with him. He doesn't have that coming."

He slowed the engine. The club's docks were ahead now. Most of the larger boats were gone, but a few motorboats were tied down and covered with tarps. The rain had caught up with them and was starting to spatter the deck.

"What are we going to find in there?" Colin asked.

Melissa shook her head. "Normal night, Frank would have the bar. A couple of Ellis's boys in the back screwing around. With the storm, I don't know. I could just walk in and see how it lays any other night. But if they know what's up...I don't know. But you sure as hell can't show your face. It'll have to be me."

"No," said Colin. "You can't go in alone. We both go in. We're not coming back here, any of us. Doesn't matter if we burn some bridges on the way out."

Melissa fell silent and looked over the side into the dark water. She might not like it, but it was the truth. Her life here was over.

They coasted into a slip, and Colin jumped to the dock. He quickly moored *Pegasus* and helped Melissa up. Then they headed up the walkway toward the club. The storm might be growing outside, but inside the party was still going full steam. Colin could hear the band playing as they approached the doors.

Melissa opened them, and the music spilled out like a wave. Faces looked up as they walked in. Colin didn't recognize them. Everyone looked lit. Someone stood with a bottle and shouted, "Welcome fellow refugees! Come ride out the mighty hurricane here with us!"

Colin pulled the door shut behind him as the wind tried to take it, and there was a wave of bawling laughter.

Despite the initial bravado, he sensed uncertainty here. There was little business at the bar, and no one was dancing to the band's tune. Most of the crowd had bottles at their tables and were drinking hard and fast. They were scared. That was good, he thought. This wasn't a good place to try and ride out a real hurricane, if that's what this was going to be. But it wasn't his job to shepherd them to safety. He had other things to worry about.

Frank was manning the bar, looking at Melissa with intensity. She walked over, and Colin followed her. Frank gave a subtle shake of his head and nodded toward Colin. Then he left someone else in charge of the bar and headed through the doors into the back.

Melissa steered him toward a stool. "Wait here," she said. "Something's up. Let me see what."

"If you don't come back fast enough, or I think something's wrong, I'm coming looking for you."

"Good," she said, "you do that."

Colin sat at the end of the bar, beside someone with the sun-wrinkled skin of a local. He signaled for a drink from the backup bartender and nodded to his new companion.

"Just got in," he said, "what's going on in town? Apart from this storm, I mean?"

The man scoffed. "You ain't heard? Somebody tried to rob Kusack's place again!"

"Again?"

"Twice in two days! Sons of bitches what they are. Sheriff got him, but..." the man looked around and leaned over with a conspiratorial gleam in his eye. "But they ain't got the money back. Still out there someplace. Got men out in this crap looking all over for it. They won't find it."

"What makes you say that?"

His new friend chuckled. "Bunch of city boys from New York? They got no idea what they're doing. Me, I'll just wait for this one to blow everything over, maybe go out and look myself."

On the speaker's far side, another man turned with a glare. "You find it, you'll damn well give it back, Tom."

"Like hell."

"Yeah, you will. Mr. Kusack ain't stupid. Not like you anyway. You'll keep your mouth shut for as long as it takes you to get in here and start bragging you're rich, and then he's going to want to have a little talk."

The would-be treasure hunter, Tom, didn't have a quick rejoinder for that.

"Besides," the newcomer added, "What do you think's going to happen if he decides he's sick of people messing with him around here? He decides Harmony Beach is too much trouble, he can pull out tomorrow and take his money to the next town down the coast. We'll be right back where we started."

Colin nodded to him. "So you're not an admirer of this fellow who robbed him, then? You don't see him as another in your great American tradition of outlaw heroes?"

The man looked at him as if he was speaking Latin. "Who the hell are you anyway?" he said after a pause.

"Nobody," Colin said with a smile. "Nobody at all."

The man glared at him for a long moment, then his beer seemed to draw his attention back to itself, inexorably, like gravity.

Colin shifted his weight off the stool and stood up. Melissa had been gone long enough. He glanced at the backup bartender, occupied at the far end of the bar. Then he slipped around the end of the bar and through the doors into the back.

He'd been here enough times when he and Stephen were running liquor to the club. The short hallway passed several storage niches, shelves lined with towels, silverware, and spare dishes. Beyond that was the door to Melissa's office, and across from it the swinging doors that led to the storeroom, and finally the stairs up to the second floor.

The howling wind made it hard to make out words, but he

heard voices from the storeroom. He recognized Melissa's. She was talking to a man. Neither voice sounded friendly.

It was time for him to stop being friendly too. Colin hadn't known what he was heading into when he left Nassau, and so he hadn't brought a gun with him. Where they were going, he was sure there would be plenty of guns. He could pick one up when he needed one. But he hadn't gone completely unarmed for some time now. He knelt down, pulled up his pants leg, and drew a long, black dagger from a sheath strapped to his right calf. The grip settled into his hand as if made for it, and he gave a brief, wry smile.

He hadn't planned on feeling that grip in his palm again. Not for business at least. He concealed the blade against his side and moved to the doors. Through the crack between them he could see crates and a pool of lantern light from the left.

"...don't give a damn," the male voice was saying. "Your boyfriend as much as said you were part of it."

"You know what he'll do to me?" Melissa said, and Colin heard fear in her voice. He edged quietly through the doors.

They were in the back corner, near the table where Kusack's hired goons usually sat playing cards. The man's back was to Colin, and Melissa looked over his shoulder. If she saw him there, she gave no reaction.

"Should have thought of that before you cheated him," the man said. He was pacing in a tight line, back and forth, his attention locked on her. "There's nothing I can do for you. Even if I wanted to."

"You like seeing me scared, don't you Eddie?" Melissa said. Colin saw her slowly raise the back of her shirt, bit by bit, with the fingers of her right hand, turning to hide the motion. Did she have a weapon?

Eddie chuckled. "I don't mind seeing Miss High and Mighty take a fall."

"Well, I got bad news for you, Eddie," she said, and the fearful tone vanished like smoke. "I was never afraid of you."

And like a striking snake, she whipped out a compact Derringer pistol and leveled it at Eddie's face. "Now put yours on the table. Nice and slow."

You're too close, Colin silently screamed at her. *Back away from him. Two steps back!*

But she didn't. She had courage all right, but she didn't have the skill to go with it. Colin started forward.

"Sure, Mel, whatever you say," said Eddie. He reached into his jacket with one hand, but then the other suddenly lashed out and slapped the gun away. She gasped and before the Derringer had stopped sliding across the floor, Eddie had drawn a .38 revolver and jammed it under her chin.

"You got a lot to pay for," he snarled.

He didn't hear Colin moving quickly up behind him, passing the knife to his left hand. Melissa had to see him, but she still gave no sign of it. *Cold when she needs to be*, he thought.

Then he did it, just like they taught him, like he thought he'd never have to do again. One hand grabbed Eddie's wrist and wrenched the gun away from her, down to the side. The pistol barked and fired a round into a crate of gin at Eddie's side. Then the blade slid in, through his jacket, under his rib cage, and into his heart. Eddie arched back, thrashed for a moment, then sank to the floor at Colin's feet.

Melissa ran to snatch up her Derringer. "You think they heard that?"

"Let's not wait to find out," Colin answered. "Out the back!"

Colin took Eddie's .38, and they hurried out the loading doors, into the storm.

"Ellis has him!" Melissa said as they hurried back toward *Pegasus*. "But he's alive. He got the money all right, but he hid it before they caught him."

Colin had gathered that much from his conversation at the

bar. That was something at least. Kusack would want his money back, so he wouldn't kill Stephen until he had it. But he'd make him damned uncomfortable to find it.

The winds were picking up. Colin felt a gust try to take him off the side of the dock as they hurried back to *Pegasus*, and the rain stung his face.

"Where will they take him?" he snapped as he helped Melissa aboard. He cast off and climbed into the cockpit himself as she thought about it.

"Back to the counting room, probably," she said. "No windows, just one way out. Separated from the rest of the house."

Colin started the engine and pulled away from the slip. He glanced back up at the club. If anyone had heard the gunshot, they hadn't decided to pursue the matter out into the storm.

"You killed Eddie," she said as they rounded the tip of the island and headed into the channel. "You just killed him."

"Yes, I did," said Colin. "It seemed the thing to do at the moment."

"No, no, I know," she said. "You had to do it, and he had it coming. I got no problem with it." She searched for the right words. "But before, it was just an idea, you understand?"

Colin nodded. "Very well. Better than you know. But now it's real. And there's probably going to be more killing before we get Stephen back. Can you deal with that? Take a second. Think about it."

She did. "Yes," she said finally. "I can handle it."

Colin believed her. For someone with no training or experience, she'd handled herself well back there. She hadn't fallen apart.

Maybe there was more to her than he'd given her credit for.

22

STEPHEN'S HEAD HURT. HE GROANED AS THE DARKNESS MELTED away into a painfully bright light.

"Yeah, you took a nasty bump to the head there," said a voice. "Then we beat you up a little more when you got here, even though you were out cold and couldn't feel it. Maybe you're feeling some of it now? Are you feeling it?"

His confusion began to recede. Sheriff Mayhew's men had caught him. Suddenly he realized exactly where he was and who was speaking to him. He was back at Kusack's house, and the man taunting him was Ellis Kusack himself.

Stephen opened his eyes again, but there was a bright lamp shining in his face, close enough that he could feel the heat on his skin now. He closed his eyes and turned away.

"Yeah, you're feeling it. Good. Hate to waste a good beating." Someone, Kusack he assumed, slapped him hard. "Where's my god damn money?"

Stephen managed to look around the glare of the lamp. He was back in the counting room, looking at the empty shelves. Kusack stood over him. Three more of his goons lurked behind him, leering. He was tied to a chair, and he could taste blood. He could localize his pain more precisely now. It wasn't just the blow to his head. They had indeed worked him over while he was unconscious. He supposed that was meant to indicate just how upset they were with him.

Kusack slapped him again. "This is the easy way, punk. What did you do with the money?"

"He didn't make it far, boss," said one of the goons behind him. "It's got to be close."

"Am I talking to you?"

"No, boss."

Kusack knelt beside Stephen. "The hard way is that I start cutting pieces off you, a little at a time. We can do that if you're going to play the tough guy. I don't mind. I like the hard way."

He reached out to grab Stephen's ear and twisted it hard. Stephen gasped.

"This just gets worse until I have my money back!"

Stephen said nothing. He knew it was the money that was keeping him alive right now. Once Kusack got it back, they'd kill him and dump his body at sea like the two men he'd seen them murder on the beach. But until then, while he might inflict a lot of pain, Kusack would keep him alive. It was a question of how much pain Stephen could take. Given the alternative, he could take a lot of pain.

"I lost it," he said. "It blew away in the storm. Sorry."

Kusack grimaced in anger, pulled back and then punched him hard in the gut. He coughed and spat blood.

Then something slammed against the outside wall. Kusack and his men all jumped. "The hell was that?" said Kusack.

"Sounded like a tree coming down," said one of the other men. "It's getting worse out there."

Kusack looked up at the ceiling, and Stephen thought he could see a bit of nervousness. The whole house was trembling in the gusts, he could feel the faint vibrations through the soles of his shoes. This was turning into a real hurricane, and that could well tear the house down around them.

Despite himself, Stephen grinned. That would sure play hell with Kusack's plan to torture him until he gave up the money.

Kusack saw the grin and shook his head. "All right," he said, "let's start with the tools then." He gestured to one of his men. "Tony, bring me the toolbox."

"Right, boss."

MELISSA KNEW a place near the mansion where a thick stand of mangroves would provide a protected anchorage, so Colin let her guide him in. It was where they'd left her boat for Stephen's escape, and that gave him pause. Stephen would have headed there, but he never made it. So they might have found the boat, or they might have beaten the location out of him by now. It was possible the spot was being watched. But the storm was growing stronger by the minute, whipping up the waves and tearing branches from the trees. Outside in this storm was no place to be. It was most likely they'd retreated back to the house.

"My boat's gone!" Melissa said as they came in. Stephen drew the pistol he'd picked up at the club, but nothing moved in the trees or on the shoreline. Colin and Melissa tied *Pegasus* off to three different trees. The boat was as secure as they could make it, but nothing was really safe in a storm this big.

Colin quickly dug through the toolbox for things that might prove useful. He stuffed a screwdriver and a flashlight in his pockets. Then they tied down a tarp over the cockpits and hurried toward the house. Trees groaned and cracked around them. Heavy branches were down across the driveway. That was a point in their favor. Nobody would be coming from outside to reinforce the enemy.

As they neared the mansion, Colin could already see damage.

Some of the upstairs windows were broken and letting in rain. Kusack's expensive Spanish roof tiles had begun to tear away. The storm was throwing them around like bullets.

They kept close to the garage for cover and moved closer to the house. Down the hill, the boathouse roof had collapsed, crushing whatever was moored there. *Fianna* hadn't been docked at the club, and Colin didn't see her here. Perhaps she was picking up rum from Cuba or had been moved safely out of the storm's path. That was too bad. Colin wouldn't have minded seeing the yacht wrecked.

Getting into the house proved surprisingly easy. On the beach side of the house was a long gallery of tall windows looking out to sea. The wind had thrown palm fronds into them, shattering the glass. The rain whipped through the jagged frames and pooled on the floor, soaking the expensive carpet. Nobody was around to challenge them as they simply stepped through an empty frame and into the hallway.

Melissa gestured toward the far end of the hall, where a doorway hung open to the storm. "Stephen was going to come in there," she said. "Down past the kitchen. Next door is the hall to the counting room."

The kitchen was dark and empty. Hanging pans rattled as the storm shook the house. Colin swept the room with his pistol, then they moved on. At the next door, Melissa stopped. "This is it."

Colin couldn't understand why Kusack didn't have someone watching this door. "Where is everybody?" he asked. "I thought Kusack had a small army here."

"He must have them out looking for the money."

"In this?" Colin was incredulous. It wasn't as if it was going anywhere with Stephen captured.

"Oh, yeah," said Melissa. "You don't know Ellis."

"You do. What are we going to find behind that door?"

Melissa shrugged. "Nothing like this ever happened before. I *think* this is where he'll take Stephen. Wherever Stephen is, I know he'll be there himself. He won't let anyone else handle it. But he'll have a few of the boys around. He likes an audience."

Colin nodded. She'd told him all she could. From here, they would just have to take things as they came.

The door past the kitchen was closed, but light came from beneath it. Melissa had described a short corridor, maybe ten steps, then a left turn and another ten steps to the counting room door. If the lights were on, someone might be waiting, perhaps outside the door where Kusack was going about his nasty business.

"Stand here," he whispered to Melissa, moving her against the wall and away from the door. Then he knelt, the pistol in one hand, and slowly turned the knob. There was no reaction, so he risked inching the door open. He held the pistol beneath his chin, ready to thrust the muzzle through the gap and fire.

But again, nothing. This part of the hall was empty. He slowly opened the door and beckoned Melissa to follow him in.

Two lamps in the ceiling lit the short hallway. There was a third at the corner, and Colin assumed there would be two more in the other leg. A switch was set in the wall near the door. Colin leaned in to whisper in Melissa's ear.

"Is there another switch at the far end?"

She thought for a moment and nodded.

Then Colin heard movement from around the corner. It was only a footstep, a creaking floorboard that sounded different from the moaning of the house in the wind. But it was real. There was someone around the corner, guarding the far door. They had to get past him, ideally without alerting the armed men Melissa said would be in there with Kusack and Stephen.

He looked at the switch again and had an idea. He whispered to Melissa again. "When I say so, I want you to flick that switch, all right? On and off, as fast as you can. Keep doing it until I tell you to stop, okay?"

She clearly didn't understand why he wanted that, but she nodded and placed her hand on the switch. Colin hoped the flickering light would confuse the guard long enough for him to close the distance between them, especially if he took it for the storm taking out the power. If nothing else, it would keep Melissa safely out of the way.

He put the pistol in his belt where he could reach it if needed, and then drew his knife. When he was ready, he nodded to Melissa. "Go!"

The hall was plunged into darkness, and he heard a sound from around the corner. Then the lights blinked on and off around him as Colin sprinted down the hall and threw himself around the corner. In a flash, he saw the guard, confused, trying to flip his own switch. By the next flash, he'd sensed Colin coming and was turning to meet him. Colin noticed a Tommy Gun leaning against the wall in the corner. The guard sprang for it, but it was too late.

Then Colin was on him, turning him away from the door. They collided, hit the wall, and Colin took him down to the floor. In a moment, the knife had done its work. Colin stood over him, the light still flickering. It was like being at the cinema, except every frame was the terrified face of the man he'd just killed.

He walked back and told Melissa she could stop.

She saw blood on his shirt. "Oh God, are you all right?"

"It's not mine."

"Oh," she said, realizing what he'd done. Then she nodded and walked up to him. He handed her the .38 he'd taken at the club.

"We're going to go in and cover the room, all right? You stay behind me and to my left. Don't fire unless I do. But if I do, then you shoot anybody who isn't me or Stephen. You got it?"

"I understand."

Colin took the guard's Tommy Gun and checked it out. It had the hundred round drum magazine, fully loaded. These guys didn't do anything by halves. He hefted it, let the weight become familiar in his hands.

"Ready?" he asked Melissa. "Here we go."

Then he drew back and kicked the door open.

He was through before anyone could react, the Tommy Gun's muzzle leveled at the figures at the other side of the room. He counted three standing, and Kusack leaning over the bloody and battered form of his brother.

Behind him, he heard Melissa gasp.

"Don't try it!" Colin shouted at one of the men who was trying to draw a pistol from his coat. The man froze.

"Anybody does something dumb and you all die. You hear me, Kusack?"

"Do what he says," said Kusack.

"Everybody move over there." He gestured with the muzzle. "Leave your guns on the table. You all right, Stephen?"

Stephen raised his head and looked up through bleary eyes. "Colin? What are you doing here?"

"What the hell do you think?"

Kusack and his men stood in a cluster in the corner. There were four pistols on the table, but one of them might have kept back a second gun. He kept them covered as he collected the pistols. There was a toolbox on the floor and a couple bloody blades on the table.

"Cut him loose," he told Melissa.

She moved behind him to Stephen's side, and he heard her gasp. "Oh, baby, what did they do to you?"

"I'm all right," said Stephen.

"You're making a big mistake here," said Kusack. "Your brother's already in deep. Now you."

"Yeah, well I've got the big gun."

Kusack smiled. "Right now, sure. So I'll make a deal. Get him to give up the money, and you can take him and go. We'll call it even."

"Screw you!" Stephen blurted from the chair. Colin ignored him.

"I don't think so."

"Best you're going to get. Like you said, right now, you got the gun. Deal's just going to get worse from here."

"Not if I just cut you down right there."

Kusack shook his head. "No, that's the worst move you can make."

"Yeah, why's that?"

Kusack just grinned and winked at Stephen.

"One way to find out, sport."

Melissa had Stephen out of the chair. He tried to stand but wobbled on his feet and went down. Melissa helped him up and this time he stood. But Colin could see he'd had it rough.

Colin gestured to the chair. "Kusack, you get that one. The rest of you, drag those other chairs over here."

They arranged the chairs in a square, all of them facing each other. Kusack had helpfully brought along plenty of rope, wire, and a couple pairs of handcuffs in his "toolbox." Colin covered them while Melissa tied them into the chairs.

"Can you move?" Colin asked Stephen, who was stretching out joints and gingerly probing his bruises.

"Nothing broken," he said. "I hurt like hell, but yeah. I'll damn well walk out of this place."

There was a loud bang from the far end of the house, and the room was plunged into total darkness. Kusack's men started yelling.

Colin turned on the flashlight he'd taken from the boat and played it across the chairs. He'd been afraid someone would take the opportunity to grab Melissa, but she was behind the last chair, its occupant's arms threaded through the back. She had a length of rope, but Colin slid her a pair of handcuffs from the toolbox.

"Use these. We've got to move."

He'd wondered how long the power would stay on in this storm. On balance he decided this was a good thing. It would be harder to navigate the darkened house, but the darkness would also hamper any pursuers.

There was another loud impact as something hit the walls, and the house shuddered. Kusack was going to find out just what a hurricane was capable of. Colin wondered how much of his palace would still be standing in the morning.

"Melissa, help Stephen, and follow my light," he said, and he started toward the door.

"I'm not done with you, Ridley!" Kusack shouted from the darkness. "This isn't over."

Colin heard the wind howling around the house, felt it shake in the storm. If they wanted to escape, they'd need to take *Pegasus* out into this.

No, it was a long way from over.

RAINWATER SLOSHED IN THE LONG GALLERY AS THEY MADE THEIR way back out from the counting room. The wind hit Colin like a fist. The windows overlooking the sea were nearly all gone now, and the storm was lashing the interior walls. The doors to the main dining room had blown open.

Still, no one was here. He knew Kusack had a dozen men or more here. What were they doing? Were they simply hunkered down somewhere hoping the house didn't collapse on them? If they were actively trying to save the house, the main portion must be in even worse shape than this.

"How are we getting out?" Stephen asked. "You come in *Pegasus*?"

"Yeah."

"Can she handle this?"

Colin didn't answer. It was madness to take a boat out to sea in this. But they had several more immediate problems to deal with before they reached that one. He didn't know if she was still there. The storm could well have uprooted trees and dropped one on her, or else torn her loose and blown her out into the channel to sink. He'd seen boats end up half a mile inland after a big hurricane. He didn't even know if they could make it safely through the storm-battered woods to reach her.

So here they were, trapped between the storm on one side and Kusack's men on the other. It was just a matter of time before one of Kusack's people got loose, or someone came looking for him. Either way, the whole house would erupt like a nest of angry wasps, storm or no storm.

"Don't really want to go out into that," said Stephen.

"I've got an idea," Melissa said suddenly. She reached out for the flashlight. "Follow me."

She led them deeper into the house. Stephen leaned on her, and Colin covered them with the Tommy Gun. Colin worried they'd run into the staff, but they only heard the occasional shout from somewhere in the darkness. Melissa led the way upstairs to the second floor and stopped, one hand over the light to shield it.

"Ellis's office is up here. There might be someone."

"Why are we going there?" Stephen asked.

"Because no one will look there. They'll figure we took off into the storm. That's where they'll look for us."

Colin had heard worse ideas. But if someone was in the office, it would mean unnecessary confrontation. "There's plenty of rooms up here. Why the office?"

"Because there's something there we can use."

She led them down the hallway, along a long and intricately woven rug, and stopped at a pair of double doors.

"In here."

Colin positioned her and Stephen off to one side, then readied the Tommy Gun and opened the door.

The office was dark, lit only by the pale light from a panoramic window that had somehow remained intact so far. His eyes swept the room, taking in furniture and a moving figure.

"Who's that?" a voice asked. It wasn't a challenge. Colin heard more fear than anything else. "That you, boss?"

The man was walking toward them. Colin strode rapidly to meet him in the middle of the room. "Nope."

Then Colin slammed the man in the jaw with the butt of the Tommy Gun, and he dropped to the floor without a sound.

Melissa and Stephen hurried in and closed the door. She swept the light around the room. Kusack's office was luxuriously appointed in leather and oak. It looked like a London banker's office. There was a huge desk that faced the window, a sidebar with glasses and bottles, an expensive looking leather sofa on one wall, and bookshelves on the other. A portrait of Kusack hung facing the door as visitors came in. He looked very pleased with himself in a suit standing beside a table with one hand on a map of his Florida kingdom.

"Let's block those doors," Colin said. Stephen helped him drag the sofa in front of them. When they had it in place, Colin sat Stephen down on it.

"Get some rest," he said gently. "Catch your breath."

Stephen nodded. "Thanks for coming. Guess I screwed up this time."

Colin grinned. "Eh, you've done worse," he lied.

Stephen took his hand. "Sure, lots of times. Besides, I knew my big brother would come bail me out."

"It's what I do."

Colin turned to see Melissa at the bookshelves, running her fingers intently down the spines. The shelves were lined with what looked like leather-bound classics of literature and philosophy. They didn't seem very suggestive of Ellis Kusack, and it occurred to him that they probably came with the polished oak shelves.

"Somewhere here," Melissa muttered to herself. "Hey, can you get that light over here? You're going to love this if I can find it."

Colin played the light across the spines. "Yes!" Melissa said suddenly. "This one."

She pulled out a thick book and reached behind it. There was a solid thunk, and Melissa swung the bookcase inward. "Check it out. Ellis's little bolt hole."

Colin pointed his light through the gap and lit up what looked like the interior of a bank vault. The space beyond was about ten feet on a side with metal walls, floor, and ceiling. The only furniture was a plush armchair with a small side table. Beside the door was a set of shelves with supplies. Colin saw weapons, food and water, and more.

"He wanted an escape tunnel," Melissa said, "because Capone has one, he said."

Colin knew perfectly well that a tunnel wouldn't work in this kind of terrain. Anyone who grew up this close to the sea would have known that. Apparently Kusack didn't.

"But, you know," said Melissa. "So he settled for this. Walls are bulletproof. Close the door and the bookcase hides it. You can lock it from inside."

"It's perfect," said Colin. "Stephen! Get over here!"

He stepped in and shone the light around. There was room for the three of them. He saw air vents in the ceiling. It was as safe a place as they were likely to find. And Kusack hadn't spared any expense. Colin saw what looked like a Regimental Medical Officer's First Aid Kit, or the American equivalent. He looked through it and found everything from splints to morphine shots.

Stephen hobbled over and let out a low whistle. "Dibs on the chair," he said and settled heavily into it.

"One more thing," Melissa said. "You got any tools?"

Colin offered her the screwdriver he'd brought from the boat, and she took it. She led him back into the office and crossed to the desk. "Shine your light over here." She found a heavy marble ash tray and used it and the screwdriver to smash the lock on a drawer.

"There's a false bottom in here," she said. "Ellis shouldn't have had me up here so much."

She did something Colin didn't see and then pulled out a thin wooden panel and tossed it to the floor. Next she came out with a large book, a ledger from the looks of it.

"Come see," she said as she laid it out on the blotter and opened it.

Colin shone the light on the pages and saw long columns of names and numbers stretching down the pages.

"That's Ellis's handwriting," Melissa said. "He doesn't trust anybody else to keep track of it. There's all his money. Where it comes from, where it goes. Payoffs to cops and judges. Companies nobody knows he owns. The whole thing."

Colin whistled. If she was right, in the right hands that book could take Kusack's whole empire apart. And Colin had a pretty good idea whose hands those would be.

"We take it with us, right?" said Melissa.

"You bet we do," Colin answered.

He took out his knife and strode to the sofa, then fell to one knee and plunged the knife into a cushion.

"What are you doing?" Melissa asked as he slashed through the leather.

Colin cut out a large rectangle of leather and ripped it free. "Making it waterproof," he said.

Melissa brought the book to him, and they carefully wrapped it up and tied it off with some packaging twine Melissa found in a desk drawer. When they were done, Colin thought it had as good a chance of surviving the storm as possible.

Outside, the storm was like a wild beast clawing at the house. The roof rattled above them as tiles ripped free. The window shook as if someone was physically throwing themselves at it. Colin wondered why it was still in one piece, then realized it was probably bulletproof glass.

"This is getting worse," he said. "Let's get inside."

They headed into Kusack's emergency sanctuary, and Colin swung the heavy door shut. It was meant to protect Kusack from his enemies, but it would do well enough. The storm was their enemy now.

Melissa lit the other battery lights, and Stephen had found the painkillers in the first aid kit.

"What's that?" Stephen asked, nodding toward the leather-wrapped bundle.

"You wanted to kill Kusack?" Colin said as he clicked the lock shut. "This might be better."

OUTSIDE THE STORM raged and howled. Inside Kusack's vault, they could hear it taking the house apart around them, but nothing could reach them. Stephen let the kit's painkillers slowly put him to sleep while Melissa carefully tended to him.

Colin inventoried the weapons on Kusack's shelves, kept an eye on his watch, and listened to the storm. They were safe here for now, but they were also trapped. If they stayed here too long, the storm would pass and Kusack's men would regroup. They'd be caught here like rats in a hole. They had to leave before the storm died down, and Colin didn't know when that would happen. But certainly they had to be gone before daylight.

It was almost three in the morning, and Colin was about to wake Stephen and get them moving when the whole room pitched to one side. Colin barely kept his feet, Melissa cried out, and Stephen jerked awake as his chair slid into the wall.

The room was off level now, by a good twenty degrees Colin estimated. The floor must have begun to collapse beneath them, or else a wall had given way and pitched the vault to one side. Either way, it wasn't good. He found himself wondering how much the vault weighed, and what would happen to them if it fell through the floor to the ground.

"What's going on?" Stephen asked.

"Time to go," said Colin.

He gave them both Colt .45 automatics from Kusack's weapons shelf. Then he unlocked the door. The vault had shifted to the left as he faced the door. At least it hadn't tilted toward the door or away from it. He just hoped it hadn't been blocked by some falling beam.

"Lights out," he told them when he had his hand on the latch. They switched off the battery-powered lanterns, and the vault was plunged into total darkness.

"No shooting, even if someone's out there, okay? I'm in the middle."

Then he pushed the heavy door open.

He was instantly slapped by a wave of warm rain, and the wind screamed over the gap in the vault. He was looking out into the storm through a jumble of shattered wood and plaster. There was a tilted floor to his left, but just yawning space to the right and a drop to the ground. The ground was littered with debris—tiles from the roof, torn pieces of wall, and broken glass. Kusack's house was a shattered wreck.

He tested the floor to the left. It held, so he stepped out. "Come out to the left!" he shouted back, then turned to catch Melissa's hand and help her out. A gust of wind hit them, and Melissa caught herself against what remained of the office wall. A small piece of wood whipped between them like a bullet and vanished into the night.

"Good God!" she said. "It's not safe out here!"

Colin couldn't argue with that. He helped Stephen out and they looked for a way down. Not safe didn't begin to describe it, Colin thought. If the wind didn't blow them out of the house, or if they weren't killed by flying debris, or if the house didn't collapse beneath them, there was still the matter of Kusack and his men. He wondered what had happened to them. The house wasn't providing much in the way of shelter anymore. Were they out in the storm? Had they fled entirely?

"Here!" Stephen called out. The staircase wasn't reachable. It had canted away from the floor and tottered at the brink of collapse a good ten feet from the edge of the floor. But the floor itself sloped down to a couple feet from the ground now where a supporting column had been knocked out. Colin guessed that was what had thrown the vault off level.

Stephen went down first, sliding down the soaked carpet. Then Melissa followed, Kusack's leather-wrapped ledger clutched tightly to her chest. Colin covered them with the Tommy Gun, though he doubted he could hit anything much more than twenty feet away in these winds. Finally he lowered the gun and slid down to join them.

The ruins of the house seemed abandoned. It was hard to imagine anyone still lurking in here.

"What do you suppose happened to Ellis and his boys?" Melissa asked as they moved out of the wreckage toward the open space of the drive. One of Kusack's Cadillacs lay over-turned, its windshield smashed. They sheltered behind it, though it didn't provide much protection. Rain drummed on the metal, and they had to shout to be heard.

"The wind's shifted!" Melissa yelled. "The center's gone past!"

She was right, Colin realized. The winds were blowing from the land out to sea now. The storm was a huge cyclone, spinning counter-clockwise. That meant the eye had passed to the north of Harmony Beach, and they were in the tail end of it now. That was something at least. But then a flying tile smashed into the Cadillac's chassis near Colin's head and shattered into tiny fragments. Two feet to the right, and it would have fractured his skull.

The storm was still dangerous. They couldn't stay here. He started to work out the safest way back to *Pegasus*.

"The garage looks intact!" Stephen shouted. He was crouched behind the car's rear end. "Wait here."

He moved out from behind the car and headed across the drive in a low crouch.

"The garage!" Melissa said. "I didn't even think about that. It's all cement block."

Cement block. Kusack might be a rube from up north who thought he could dig tunnels through the beach, but someone would have told him he needed a hurricane shelter. That's where he and his men would be.

He leapt up and looked over the Cadillac's body. "Stephen! Come back!"

Too late.

A door opened at the end of the garage, and a figure stepped into the wedge of lantern light that spilled from it. Then came muzzle flashes and the chatter of a Tommy Gun. Stephen whirled and sprinted back toward the cover of the car.

He rounded the corner and fell into a crouch behind the rear wheels. He grinned up at Colin.

"Found them!"

24

THEY RAN BACK TOWARD THE HOUSE AS KUSACK'S MEN BOILED OUT of the garage. Colin heard gunfire, but at this range the wind would take the bullets God only knew where. Colin was more afraid of the storm. Kusack's soldiers didn't seem to understand that. They were firing wildly, charging through the wind and rain after them.

"Stay together!" Colin shouted as they ducked around a partially collapsed wall into what had once been a grand entry foyer. Melissa led. She at least knew how the house had been laid out before the storm got to it.

"Where are we going?" Melissa shouted back.

"Out to the construction!" Stephen answered. "Up that bank to the trees. Then we can circle around to the boat. I can find where I buried the money!"

"Are you crazy?" Colin asked. "We don't have time to go treasure hunting right now!"

"I know right where it is!"

"Leave it! For Christ's sake!"

"This way boys," said Melissa. She'd found a corridor that was mostly intact, although one wall canted dangerously over, giving the hall an almost triangular cross section. They were out of the worst of the wind here, but it was a long stretch of hall that channeled them into a straight line. They'd be easy targets here.

Colin turned and walked backward, watching the end where they'd entered. Sure enough, a figure appeared, raising a weapon.

Colin opened up with the Tommy Gun and cut him down. He heard shouts, and bullets began piercing the thin interior walls around them.

"Go!" he shouted. "Move it!"

Stephen and Melissa hurried down the hall, and Colin followed as quickly as he could. Another figure spun around the edge of the wall and fired at them. Colin traded fire with him, hearing bullets rip into the walls around him.

He risked a quick look over his shoulder and saw Stephen and Melissa clearing the far end of the hall. He fired one more long burst back down the corridor to keep his attacker under cover, then turned and ran out after them.

Again the wind ripped at his clothes, and the rain stung his skin. This wing had been under construction and was even more chaotic than the rest of the house. Timbers jutted at odd angles, and overturned scaffolds were festooned with wildly flapping palm fronds. The wind whipped plywood sheets against cement forms. It sounded like war. He saw Stephen and Melissa a few yards ahead, making their way through the chaos toward a sandy slope that led up into trees.

Then there was a blur of motion from the left, and figures flew out of the wreckage. One dove at Melissa as she tried to raise her pistol. They spun together, her back slamming against a wall. The second figure sprinted at Stephen, and Colin recognized Kusack.

Kusack hit Stephen low from the side and bore him to the ground. They rolled together amid the debris. Colin raised the Tommy Gun but knew he didn't dare take a shot with Stephen so close. Instead he raised the butt to club the man on Melissa. But as he prepared to strike, her pistol went off. It fired once, then twice more, and her attacker fell back and spun to the ground in a heap. She looked down at him in horror, then to Colin as if to ask what she'd done.

Beyond her, he saw Kusack sink a vicious punch into Stephen's midsection. "Where's my money, you son of a bitch," Kusack snarled.

Stephen managed to kick him off, and Kusack stumbled backward to his feet. He drew back to launch a kick into Stephen's ribs. Colin was moving to take Kusack down when he heard a horrible ripping sound from behind. He turned to see a large plywood sheet tear free from its framing. It flipped over what looked like the edge of a swimming pool, and pinwheeled toward him. He dropped the gun and dove for Melissa. He tackled her, and they hit the ground as the sheet tumbled through the air above them.

Kusack saw it coming, but too late. Before he could move, the sheet took him in the forehead and threw him back into a support beam with a sickening crack. He tumbled limp to the ground and didn't move. His face was covered in blood, black in the dim light.

Maybe Kusack was dead, maybe he wasn't. It didn't matter right now.

"Bring the book!" he shouted at Melissa, then hurried to help Stephen up.

"I'm okay," Stephen said, "Okay."

"That's great," Colin answered, "let's get out of here!"

They made their way up the slope and into the trees. They hurried under the cover of the forest until they had to cross the drive. Then they made their way back through the woods toward *Pegasus*. Or at least where Colin hoped he'd find his boat. It was slower going now. Trees and branches were down everywhere and more swayed and creaked in the wind, threatening to come down on them. More than once they heard the loud crack of wood giving way and the sounds of trunks crashing down through the branches.

At last Colin started to recognize landmarks. They were close to the shore, near the mangroves. Then he saw the dim shape of the canvas tarp against the darker background. *Pegasus* was still there. They hurried to the boat and Colin saw how lucky they'd been. A tree had been uprooted and had fallen no more than a couple feet from the boat. But *Pegasus* was intact, still moored down and afloat, though the tarp was scattered with fallen branches.

Melissa removed the tarp while Stephen and Colin moved more fallen branches out of the way to clear their path out of the grove. Then they all grabbed the gunwales and walked the boat out toward deeper water. When he thought they had enough draft, Colin helped Melissa aboard, then Stephen.

Colin was climbing aboard himself when he heard shouts behind him, and muzzle flashes lit up the night. Kusack's men were still in the fight, and somehow they'd found them. Someone must have remembered that Melissa's boat had been left here and guessed they'd come back.

"Start the motor!" he shouted at Stephen as Melissa helped pull him up and over the side. A moment later the Napier Lion sprang to life. Colin tumbled into the cockpit, falling against Melissa and pushing her into Stephen's lap. He saw half a dozen men charging out into the shallow water among the mangroves. They were firing as they came, but the wind drove their shots wild. Colin saw Joe Stoski in the lead. With Kusack out of action, he must have taken charge.

Then a bullet creased the hull beside Colin, and he dropped down into his seat. They could still get a lucky shot, and they were coming closer. It was time to go.

Colin put the boat into reverse and slammed the throttle open, praying some fallen trunk wasn't waiting just beneath the surface to rip out the bottom. *Pegasus* lurched back, and Colin steered between the last of the trees, out into the open channel. Stoski and his men fell behind, still firing uselessly into the teeth of the storm. Colin turned and switched the engine back to forward. The propeller ground up the water, and they took off away from the shore.

The water was rough, the wind whipping the surface into whitecaps. The boat pitched and slammed through the waves.

"Where are we going?" Melissa shouted.

There was only one place to go, though it would be even rougher and more dangerous than the relatively protected waters of the channel. The channel was too shallow and too narrow. Already the wind was trying to drive them back toward the shore. And once again, there was nowhere safe for them to go along the coast, nowhere Kusack's remaining men couldn't follow them.

The idea terrified him, but he didn't see a choice. They had to risk going out into open water.

"Out to sea!" he shouted back. "Try and run south, get out of it!"

Melissa blanched. She knew as well as he did how dangerous this storm would be in the open sea. But she also realized there was no place else to go. Stephen nodded.

"Let's do it."

Colin headed down toward the island's southern tip. They would swing around the ruins of the mansion and head out to sea.

And then heaven help us, he thought.

KUSACK'S MEN tried to fire on them as they passed the house. Colin saw muzzle flashes from the dock that led around to the boathouse. But it wasn't gunfire he was worried about. The sea was much heavier here, outside the protective shield of the island. As they cleared the channel, Colin could see the waves surging up the beach, flooding Kusack's partially constructed pool and undermining the foundations. By morning he doubted there would be anything left of the house at all.

He left the house to its fate and concentrated on staying alive. The waves were a frenzy of white water all around them, and the wind kept trying to turn *Pegasus* off course. As they got farther out, she began to pitch as she cleared the wave crests and then fell down into the next trough. The bow would lurch into the air then smash back down to the surface again.

Eventually a hull would be broken apart by that continuous pounding. He knew *Pegasus'* construction was sound, but even a hull that well-built had its limits. He just hoped they could outrun the storm before they reached them.

If the storm was north of them and heading west, then the shortest route out of it would be southeast. Colin steered that way, or as much as he dared. The most important thing now was to keep the bow into the waves. If he turned too far to the side, the waves would throw the boat sideways and eventually capsize her.

He glanced over at Stephen and Melissa, crammed together in a seat meant for one. There were seats in the forward area of course, but it was madness to try and get there in this weather. And they needed each other close, he realized. They were both terrified, holding tight to each other for comfort. He couldn't blame them. He could use someone to hold right now.

Stephen looked astern and suddenly shouted, "You've got to be kidding me!"

Colin looked back and was astonished to see lights. There was a boat back there, chasing them. It could only be Kusack's people.

"I guess they really want that money back."

"Got to be Joe Stoski," said Melissa. "He's like a dog with a bone once he gets onto something."

"What the hell do they think they're doing?" said Stephen. "It's crazy."

Kusack's men were gangsters from up north, city men who knew little about boats and less about how dangerous a hurricane could be. They probably had no idea how much danger they'd put themselves in.

"They don't know what they're doing!" Colin shouted.

Stephen grinned for a moment. "Okay, what's our excuse?"

"We're desperate!"

The other boat was actually closing on them, Colin saw now, the lights moving steadily closer as they vanished behind a wave then reemerged. They were pushing their boat to its limit, harder than he dared.

Even so it would take them some time to catch up. Hopefully he'd have some idea what to do by then. A wave caught *Pegasus* at an angle and threw them over to one side. Colin slammed painfully against the side of the cockpit. He winced and turned back into the waves before the next one could roll them.

They made perhaps another mile, the other boat steadily closing on them. They were persistent, and brave, Colin admitted. It took courage to take a boat into this, even if they weren't fully aware of how much danger they were in.

He looked down and saw water sloshing around the cockpit, nearly to his ankles. Between the rain and spray, they were taking on water fast. If it got to the engine, they'd be helpless before the storm. Melissa and Stephen were looking back, watching the chase boat with a grim intensity. He elbowed Stephen to get his attention.

"Find something and start bailing! We have to keep water out of the engine!"

Stephen nodded, and he and Melissa found a funnel and an empty tin can. They got to work as best they could in the cramped cockpit. Of course the same thing would be happening in the forward areas they couldn't get to. Colin tried not to think of that.

After a few more minutes of pounding, he glanced back over his shoulder. Stoski's boat was much closer now. He made out two figures up on the bow. They were moving carefully, on hands and knees. They must have secured themselves to the boat somehow.

Then *Pegasus* slid down a trough, and he lost sight of the other boat for a moment. When it reappeared, the men on the bow opened up with Tommy Guns. He saw the muzzle flashes and heard the guns' faint chatter even through the howling of the wind. One lucky bullet thunked into the stern. The winds made aiming next to impossible, but if they got close enough…

"Stay down!" he shouted to Stephen and Melissa. Then a wave slammed the bottom of the hull and there was a terrible lurch as *Pegasus* went airborne for a moment and smashed hard into the water. The sea broke over the bow, and Colin was nearly pulled from the cockpit. He glanced down at Stephen and Melissa. They were soaked, but all right. He felt the boat lumbering under the new weight of the water they'd taken on. She was close to foundering.

Then the Lion engine sputtered and died.

Colin's heart dropped. They were going to die out here. He'd been foolish to think they could survive this. If the storm didn't kill them, Stoski's men would. At least they might take Stephen back with them to recover the money. He'd live a little longer. But not very long, and it wouldn't be pleasant.

He shook off his fear as best he could and tried to restart the engine.

Then he realized he didn't hear the guns anymore.

Colin stood up and looked around, holding tight to the wheel as *Pegasus* tossed in the waves. There was no sign of the boat pursuing them. It had simply vanished, as if the sea had swallowed it whole. That was exactly what had happened, Colin real-

RUMRUNNERS

ized after an astonished moment. They'd turned wrong into a wave, gone under and not come back up. Or perhaps the pounding had broken up their hull. Maybe Stoski and his crew had watched as it came apart around them and dropped them into the sea.

Either way, they were gone, as if they'd never been there at all. There was nothing but the fierce waves, the lashing rain, and the wind. Of course, that was more than enough.

"What happened?" Melissa asked. "What do we do?"

"Sea anchor!" Colin shouted. It was a rope with a series of canvas shrouds like so many umbrellas. It was crumpled up in a compartment beneath the seats. Colin had never had reason to use it before, but now was the time. Dragging behind the stern, it would act as a brake and help keep the bow pointed into the waves. That was their only hope now, to keep afloat and ride the sea until the storm passed over them.

Stephen and Melissa helped him get the sea anchor out and deploy it.

Then they bailed and prayed their own silent prayers to whatever power could protect them as the night wore on, and the storm tossed them around the sea.

25

PEGASUS SAT ON THE FLAT, GLASSY SEA THE NEXT MORNING LIKE A sodden leaf. The sun gleamed bright on the water. The storm had passed in the night, and the morning was calm. It was like the battlefields when the guns fell silent, Colin thought. The sudden silence after so much howling destruction. No one had moved or said a word. They barely dared to breathe for fear that the stillness would break, erupt into howling death once more. It had sounded like this.

He sat up and looked into the morning sun. It occurred to him that he was alive, *Pegasus* was still afloat, the storm was gone, and his brother and Melissa were still in the cockpit beside him. Somehow, they'd made it.

He gently roused them, and they all looked at the flawless morning sky and the calm sea with amazement.

"What do we do now?" Melissa finally asked.

Colin looked down at the water, nearly up to the level of the seats. *Pegasus* had nearly foundered. The top deck was barely a foot above the surface. The water in the forward spaces and the engine compartment would be as bad. That was the first thing to deal with.

"We bail," he said, and they quietly got to work.

While they bailed, Colin considered their situation. If he could get the engine cleared and working, it would be simple enough to go to shore. If he couldn't, they'd be at the mercy of the currents. Here, they would be swept farther out to sea with no radio to call for help. It was a long way to Europe.

No, he told himself, that wouldn't happen. The Lion had kept running with a bullet in it. There was no reason to think there was any mechanical damage this time. If they got the water out, it should run.

"I'm going forward," he told them. "Get started up there."

"Hey, Colin," Stephen said as he was climbing up onto the upper deck. He stopped and looked back.

"Thanks. For coming to get me."

Colin nodded. "Don't mention it." Then he headed forward and began scooping water out of the cargo space.

It was Colin who first saw the speck on the horizon. He thought it must be a ship, but he didn't mention it to the others. There was no reason to think the crew had seen them, and they had no way to signal for help.

But the speck grew larger and resolved into a hull with a single stack and a tall mast. Stephen and Melissa saw it now, and in a moment Melissa was up on deck waving her arms and shouting.

It wouldn't hurt, Colin decided, but he was reasonably sure now that they'd been spotted.

As the ship steamed closer, Colin recognized her. He sat down on the deck, shook his head, and laughed. It was the *Mojave*, out searching for survivors of the storm.

The cutter pulled alongside, and a flurry of activity broke out on deck. Sailors descended to the *Pegasus* on ropes with bosun's chairs and got all three of them aboard. They lowered hoses and began pumping the remaining water out of *Pegasus*. Colin,

Stephen, and Melissa were hurried below for another medical exam.

It was nearly an hour before they found themselves once again in the same cabin they'd been brought to the last time the *Mojave* had fished them from the sea. After a few minutes, the door opened, just as it had the last time, and Sam Blake walked in. He let the door close while he looked them over and shook his head.

"Have you boys considered that this might not be the right line of work for you? Morning, Melissa."

"Morning, Sam."

"Yeah, I think we've pushed our luck about as far as I want to push it," said Colin.

"What the hell were you doing out in that?" Blake asked, incredulous. "I know you know better."

"The alternative was the tender mercies of Ellis Kusack," said Colin. "I think under the circumstances we made the right choice."

"You were at Kusack's place?" he said, letting out a low whistle. "They say there's not a piece of it left that you couldn't fit in a sack and carry off over your shoulder. Place looks like a battlefield."

"It was," said Stephen.

Blake's curiosity was piqued at that. Colin thought it best to divert him before he asked more pointed questions.

"But I'm glad it was you that found us, Sam," he said. "We brought you something."

Stephen looked over at him, uncertainty in his face. Colin nodded. "Yeah," he said, "It's the last card. Here's where we play it."

Melissa had the book in her lap, still wrapped up tightly in leather cut from Kusack's office couch. She undid the strings and unwrapped the soaked and salt-stained leather. The book appeared to have weathered the storm more or less intact. Blake leaned on the tabletop and reached out to touch the green fabric cover.

"Well, what have you found?"

He opened it to a ledger page. The paper was pale green with blue and red lines framing columns of numbers and text entries. He turned to another random page and found more of the same.

Blake let out a low whistle. "This what it looks like?"

"Ellis's private ledger," said Melissa. "Straight from his desk."

"It's got all you need to take Kusack apart," Colin said, "if he's still alive."

Blake looked up. "What?"

"We saw him get hit by a flying chunk of his house. I don't know if it killed him. We didn't have time to check. But I wouldn't be surprised if he's buried under what's left of the place."

Blake stood up and turned for the door. "You three stay right here."

"Where's he going in such a hurry?" Melissa asked after the door closed behind him.

"Radio room, I expect," said Colin. "We just dropped a couple bombs in his lap. He'll want to report up his chain of command."

A few minutes later, Blake returned and closed the door. Again he opened to a random page and scanned down the entries. He shook his head in amazement.

"Ellis Kusack's in the hospital," he said after a moment. "Suffering from a significant head wound. He's unconscious. They don't know if he's going to wake up."

Blake turned the page and shook his head. "If he does, he's going to wish he hadn't."

"Can you use that in court?" Melissa asked. "Don't you need a warrant for it or something?"

"And we're still not testifying!" Stephen added.

Blake chuckled. "Don't worry, the last thing they'll do is put any of you on the stand. I don't know how you got this, what you were doing at Kusack's place last night, or anything else you've been up to. I don't want to know, and neither will a prosecutor. You people need to stay as far from a courtroom as you can get. Go home preferably. Out of the country. And if you see anybody that so much as looks like a defense attorney, you run. This, on the other hand, is going back to Miami as soon as we can get it there."

Blake closed the book, then picked it up and tucked it under his arm. "To answer your question," he said to Melissa, "no it won't be admissible as evidence given its...questionable history. But that's fine. This is a treasure map. It tells us where to dig, and when we start digging we'll find all the evidence we need. If Kusack makes it, he'll spend the rest of his life in jail. And the government's going to take his world apart piece by piece just like that storm did to his house."

"So what about us?" Colin asked.

Blake scoffed. "I don't even want you people back on American soil if I can help it. There's men working on your boat right now. Crew chief says she's seaworthy, which is high praise from him. You got a good boat, Ridley. Once they get her pumped dry and the engine cleared, we'll top off your tanks courtesy of the United States Coast Guard and send you on your way."

He tapped the book under his arm. "This," he said, "we'll just treat like an anonymous tip."

Colin stood to shake Blake's hand. "I think that's an arrangement we can live with."

"It better be," said Blake. "It'll be a couple hours before your boat's ready, and you all look like you could use some rest. There's a couple cabins you can use. The ensign outside will show you."

"Thank you," said Colin.

"He'll come get you when your boat's ready. Then you'll have clear skies and calm seas back to wherever you came from. It's been fun."

"Thanks, Blake," said Colin. "See you around."

Blake shook his head and grinned. "Don't take this the wrong way, but I hope to hell I never see any of you again."

As it turned out, the Coast Guard frowned on cohabitation by unmarried couples aboard their vessels. Melissa got a cabin of her own while Colin and Stephen shared another. When the door closed behind them, they both sat down on the lower of the two bunks. Colin let out a long sigh. They'd tried to maintain a front for Blake, but the truth was that they were both exhausted.

For a long minute they sat side by side in silence. Then Colin leaned back against the bulkhead and gently punched Stephen's shoulder.

"You done trying to get us all killed for a while?"

Stephen snorted. "You started it. I was running the farm."

Colin shrugged. That was true enough.

"So, what do think of a life of action and adventure? Was it everything you dreamed it would be?"

Stephen leaned forward, elbows on knees and his chin in his hands. He took a deep breath.

"You've got to watch out don't you? It gets under your skin and it's like you get drunk on it. It makes you do stupid things. Going after Kusack like that. By myself. Stupid. You were right."

"I saw it happen to men in the war. Most of us had the good sense to be scared to death. But sometimes you'd see someone who couldn't get enough. Like the war was the best thing that ever happened to them. They were like the ones who hooked themselves on morphine, except they were up all the time. They were going to fight their way into Berlin and gut the Kaiser in person."

"Well I read that he's living in Holland these days, writing his memoirs, so I guess none of those guys got him."

Colin chuckled. "No, they got killed mostly. You learned to keep clear of them. Or else they were likely to get you killed too."

Stephen leaned back beside Colin and put his hand on his. "Well, I didn't do that at least."

Colin squeezed his brother's hand. "No, no. God knows you tried."

They both laughed. "Well, we made it out in one piece anyway," said Stephen. "But I think I'll take a break from action and adventure for a while. Get to know Melissa a little better. And I don't care if you don't like her."

"Actually, I've had something of a change of heart about Melissa," said Colin.

Stephen turned to look at him in surprise. "Really? Are we talking about actual approval here?"

"Well, Kusack's out of the way for one thing. And she did all right. I didn't have to drag her back there to get you. I think she'd have gone on her own if she had to. She's brave, she's tough, and she's loyal."

"You make her sound like a Bull Mastiff," said Stephen.

"I'm saying I think she'd be good for you. It's not like you need it, but you've got my blessing if you two want each other."

Stephen was quiet. Then, "Thank you. I appreciate that. What about you? Where will you go?"

"Back to Nassau, I guess. Work the casino. Maybe see if Joe needs a mechanic."

Stephen stood up, stretched, and then climbed into the upper bunk. "There ought to be more than that after all we went through," he said. "Think about it. I'm going to get some sleep."

Colin lay back on the lower bunk. He could feel the exhaustion creeping through his bones. Yeah, he thought as sleep followed close behind it, there ought to be more to life. But in his experience there seldom was.

It would be nice, though, just once, he thought as sleep finally settled over him like a cloak.

26

NASSAU, TWO WEEKS LATER.

Colin sat on the dock outside Joe's boat shed and looked out over the water. He could hear Joe on the phone inside, shouting at someone. She'd ordered a new engine from London that clearly had not met her standards. At the moment he had nothing to do, which was actually kind of a nice feeling.

He wasn't working for Joe. She'd scoffed at the suggestion and pointed out she was already a better mechanic than he was, which Colin couldn't dispute. So she wasn't his employer, which meant she wasn't paying him. But they enjoyed each other's company, and it was something to do until he sorted things out.

When he and Stephen had returned to Beckers Cay, they found the hurricane had demolished their house as effectively as it had Kusack's. That was a sign, Colin thought. The house had faced plenty of heavy storms before and come through intact. But this time it had just given up and collapsed. Perhaps it hadn't been the construction at all, but the sheer force of Emily's will that had kept it standing. With her gone, there was no need anymore.

They'd made sure everyone else was all right. The rest of the island's population had the sense to build low and out of the worst of the winds. A couple roofs had been torn off, but nobody was hurt, and the repairs were already underway by the time they arrived.

They'd gone through the ruins of the house and managed to rescue a few mementos. Then they prepared to leave. There was nothing else here for them. The people who'd once worked on their farm didn't need them. They'd long since figured out how to live here on their own.

There was one last big party with the final remnants of their rumrunning stock. Everyone shared memories of their parents and the old days when the farm had been flush.

In the morning, they said their goodbyes and left. Colin thought Stephen and Melissa would come with him to Nassau in *Pegasus*, but they'd begged off. They'd taken one of the fishing boats and headed out on their own.

And so here he was. Free. Once he'd fled from the family farm, so desperate to get away and then to stay away. Now that was no longer an issue. He could go anywhere in the world without the strings of guilt and obligation holding him back. But here he was, sitting on Joe's dock with nowhere else to be.

It wasn't all he'd imagined if he was being completely honest with himself.

A horn sounded out on the water, and Colin glanced up to see a motor launch hurrying toward the dock. Colin recognized the livery. It belonged to a transport company that carried well-off tourists around the nearby islands. Two uniformed sailors sat up front, and two passengers in back. As they approached, Colin stood up and said to himself, "Well, I'll be damned."

The passengers in the back were Stephen and Melissa.

The boat pulled up to the dock, and Stephen started to help Melissa up, but one of the crewmen leaped to the dock, pulled the boat in close by a line, and offered Melissa an arm.

"Colin!" she said, stepping up to the dock. She gave a half spin to show off her beaded dress. "What do you think?"

Stephen was wearing a suit to complement the dress. Colin prided himself on knowing his tailoring, and he knew Stephen didn't. There were some things he might have done differently. But he also had a pretty good idea how much Stephen had spent on it.

Melissa kissed Colin's cheek as the sailor helped Stephen out of the boat.

"So where have you two been?" he asked, although he had a pretty good idea.

"Oh, here and about," said Stephen. "I'm taking Melissa to England. Show her the old family stomping grounds. Introduce ourselves to the other branch of the family, all those cousins we've never met."

"Well, that'll be nice," Colin said evenly.

"We've just got a minute, then we've got to hurry to catch a steamship," said Melissa. "It's very exciting, but we couldn't leave without saying goodbye and thanking you once more for everything."

"Don't know when we'll be back," said Stephen, "But we brought you a little parting gift."

Stephen gestured to the sailor, who had gotten back on the boat and stood waiting in the passenger compartment. He hefted a bulky canvas duffel bag and tossed it up onto the dock. It landed at Colin's feet with a heavy thud.

Colin shook his head. "Well, where'd you get that?"

"Found it on a beach, believe it or not," said Stephen with a grin. "Got a little sand in it, but it's okay. There were two of them, so we thought you might like one."

He reached out and felt the fabric of Stephen's lapel. "I see you're already putting the other one to good use."

Stephen shrugged. "Thought we should reflect our new circumstances."

Then he dropped the grin and the bantering tone. "Take care of yourself, Colin."

Colin pulled him into an embrace. "No problem," he said, "now I can get you off my back and let Melissa look after you for a while."

"We're looking after each other."

"Good plan," said Colin. Then he added, "When you get to London, go see my tailor. Anderson and Sheppard, Savile Row."

Stephen pulled back and looked him in the eye. "Jerk," he said in a playful tone. "This was a very expensive suit."

Behind them, Melissa said, "We've got to go, Stephen, or we'll be left behind. Colin, we'll send you a cable when we arrive. Where are you staying these days?"

Colin paused. He wasn't really staying anywhere at the moment. But then he looked down at the bag at his feet. That did change things a bit.

"The New Colonial," he said brightly.

Melissa laughed. "Only the best." She kissed his cheek once again, then let the sailor help her back down into the boat.

Stephen and Colin shook hands. "I'll miss you," said Stephen.

"No, you won't."

Stephen grinned. "Well, when I have a moment to myself, I will. You know, I was very angry at you for a long time."

Colin nodded.

"None of that seems to matter anymore," Stephen concluded after a moment. "The past is gone. The future's waiting out there."

"Make it a good one," said Colin.

"You too."

Stephen climbed down into the boat. The engine started, and they waved at Colin as the boat pulled away and hurried toward the steamship pier.

Colin watched the boat recede into the distance. Stephen was right. The past was gone. If Stephen had let go of it, then maybe he didn't need to keep running from it anymore.

"All right, that's that!" Joe shouted as she stomped out of the shed. "Done for the day. I'm done arguing with some lout that doesn't know a compression ratio from a flan recipe. Should have gone with the Liberty to start with. I'm done. Just done. Let's go get drunk and pick up some girls."

She tramped over to where Colin stood, still complaining about bad engines, incompetent engineers, and the shipping delay to get parts to Nassau.

"What's that?" she asked when she noticed the duffel bag at Colin's feet.

"That," he said, "is somewhere in the neighborhood of one and a half million dollars."

Joe was stopped cold. She stood still and said nothing for a good thirty seconds. Colin hadn't realized she could do that.

"No shit," she finally said. "Well, I guess you're buying."

"Yeah, fair enough."

Colin still had no idea what this new future might hold, and part of him wondered if he should be worried about that. But not right now. He could worry about that in the morning.

Right now, everything was all right.

THE END

Find more fast-moving adventure
with John Crane!

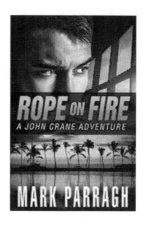

When the Hurricane Group suddenly closes shop, agent John Crane is at loose ends. Enter Josh Sulenski, a geeky Internet billionaire with a plan to save the world. All he needs is his own secret agent. Now Crane and Josh are making up all new rules for the spy game. Fans call the John Crane series "a breath of fresh air" in the espionage genre. And it all begins with *Rope on Fire*.

Available now at:
Amazon

Want even more?

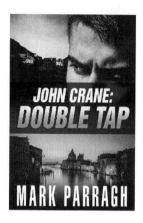

John Crane: Double Tap collects two novella-length adventures that expand John Crane's world and flesh out what happens between the first three novels.

And you can get it **free**, **right now**, when you join Mark Parragh's VIP email list. You'll get updates on new releases, sneak previews, and free bonus material available nowhere else, starting right away with your free copy of *John Crane: Double Tap*.

Join us at MarkParragh.com

CONTACT MARK PARRAGH

Mark Parragh's web site is at markparragh.com. There you can find a complete list of his books and much more. You can also find him on Facebook at facebook.com/MarkParragh, or email him at inbox@markparragh.com.

~

IF YOU ENJOYED THIS BOOK...

...please help someone else enjoy it too. Reviews are hugely important in helping readers find the books they love. Reviews help me keep writing and they make sure the books you enjoy keep coming. Just a few moments to leave a review of this book pays off in so many ways. I'd really appreciate your help.

Thank you!

— Mark Parragh